QUEEN B

"Secret magic, forbidden love, and courtly intrigue abound in this passionate and richly rendered sapphic historical fantasy. . . . This taste of the founding lore of Her Majesty's Royal Coven will delight series fans and stands well enough on its own to draw in newcomers as well. Dawson leaves readers wanting more."
—*Publishers Weekly*

"Dawson's novel sets up one woman's story of love, service, and survival and builds on her alternate England where witches and their enemies are in power. This prequel to *Her Majesty's Royal Coven* leans into the real history of Anne Boleyn and creates a delightful origin story for the series."
—*Library Journal*

THE SHADOW CABINET

"Dawson takes everything that worked so well in the first book and makes it stand out even brighter. At times provocative and sharp, at others funny and filled with queer joy, this book is sure to keep lovers of the first book very happy. Told from a variety of different characters, the threads of the story are woven together even more intricately and alliances (as well as friendships) shift as we dive deeper into this magical world. . . . As always, Dawson's talent of tackling contemporary topics in a fantastical setting truly makes this story stick with you. . . . This entrancing mix of feminism, queerness, magic, and power-hungry villains makes for an intoxicating reading experience. *The Shadow Cabinet* takes the irresistible themes of *Her Majesty's Royal Coven* and amplifies their reach well beyond the pages of the book."
—*The Nerd Daily*

"The characters that were so carefully and diligently created in the first book are given their own stories in the second book, and it is a blast to

read. . . . The complexities of modern life are here; thrown into the mix are magic, witches, and rules created around them . . . There are no limits in this fantasy world; even the established rules are pushed. Readers who enjoy feminist, queer fantasy like *The Priory of the Orange Tree* (2019) by Samantha Shannon, will enjoy this series."
—*Booklist* (starred review)

"The brilliant and fast-paced second contemporary political fantasy in Dawson's HMRC trilogy (after *Her Majesty's Royal Coven*) takes the series to new heights. . . . Dawson handles the tricky middle book with aplomb, raising the stakes and deepening the rich world-building without losing sight of the pathos that makes her characters shine. Magic seamlessly weaves with pop culture references, fun soap-operatic twists, and an incisive look at the psychology of violent misogyny. This is the work of a master storyteller."
—*Publishers Weekly* (starred review)

"The fast pace keeps the many stories moving as the points of view shift, and once again Dawson places a bombshell at the end to surprise readers. The second book of the series, after *Her Majesty's Royal Coven*, is filled with witty dialogue, pop culture references, and features the bonds of childhood, sisterhood, and fighting for what one believes in."
—*Library Journal*

HER MAJESTY'S ROYAL COVEN

"There's so much humor and sadness here, so much tenderness and compassion and a deep love of women. The book draws a gentle thread through the visions we have for ourselves, the memories from which we build our relationships and the ways in which we comprehend the present, and then it pulls that thread taut. Superb and almost unbearably charming, *Her Majesty's Royal Coven* is a beautiful exploration of how foundational friendships age, and it expertly launches an exciting new trilogy."
—*The New York Times Book Review*

"*Her Majesty's Royal Coven* is a shimmering, irresistible cauldron's brew of my favorite things: a thrilling, witchy plot; a diverse, compelling, and beautifully drawn cast; complex relationships with real heart;

laugh-out-loud banter; and the kind of dazzling magic I wish existed. You won't be able to put it down."

—Lana Harper, *New York Times* bestselling author of
Payback's a Witch

"Juno Dawson is at the top of her game in this vibrant and meticulous take on witchcraft. Her characteristic wit and grit shine through *Her Majesty's Royal Coven*, which paints a convincing picture of how magic might converge with the modern world."

—Samantha Shannon, *New York Times* bestselling author of
The Bone Season and *The Priory of the Orange Tree*

"Talk about a gut punch of a novel. *Her Majesty's Royal Coven* is sure to have readers who love witchy stories—and the queerer, the better—salivating from the very first page. . . . This book has more twists, betrayals, and drama than a *Desperate Housewives* episode and I lived for that. . . . A provocative exploration of intersectional feminism, loyalty, gender, and transphobia, Dawson's *Her Majesty's Royal Coven* is an immersive story about what it means to be a woman—and a witch—and invites readers into an intricately woven web of magic, friendship and power."

—*The Nerd Daily*

"Dawson, in an impressive flex, uses the rules of the fantasy genre to make a statement about people of color and LGBTQ individuals and how organizations can exclude and ignore them. Readers who enjoy witches and watching change ripple through a culture will enjoy this series."

—*Booklist* (starred review)

"A femme-forward story of power, morality, and fate that is not shy about its politics. . . . Beyond its politics, what especially makes *Her Majesty's Royal Coven* shine is its impeccable voice. Dawson's conversational, matter-of-fact tone calls to mind writers like Neil Gaiman and Diana Wynne Jones; it's at times funny, at others heartbreaking, but always perfectly calibrated. . . . A thoughtful entry into the witch canon that intrigues and challenges as much as it delights."

—*BookPage*

"Juno Dawson has created your new obsession. *Her Majesty's Royal Coven* is full of her trademark heart and humor, with a delicious slick of darkness. I fell in love with her coven—and I need the next installment now!" —Kiran Millwood Hargrave, author of *The Mercies*

"Such a joy to read—the world-building is incredible, the writing sophisticated, and the exploration of gender and identity is done with nuance and care. Utterly compelling."
    —Louise O'Neill, author of *Asking for It* and *The Surface Breaks*

"The funniest paranormal epic I've ever had the pleasure to read."
    —Nicole Galland, bestselling author of *Master of the Revels*

"Look if the idea of a story about a group of girls living in an alternate England and working for a centuries-old secret government bureau of witches doesn't grab you immediately, I don't know what to tell you. Except that there's also a witch civil war, an oracle that prophecies a young warlock will bring about genocide, and a group of friends torn about how to stop it." —*Paste*

"Cleverly constructed . . . a gradually building layer of political commentary ultimately reveals a complex metaphor for the UK's sociopolitical climate and mainstream transphobia. . . . An exciting new direction for Dawson. Readers will be eager for the next installment."
    —*Publishers Weekly*

"This first adult novel by YA author Dawson (*Clean; Meat Market*) is a story of feminism, matriarchy, gender roles, and tradition. . . . Readers who love a big fight between good and evil, who enjoy seeing magic in the everyday world, and those who like their heroines' journeys to include all facets of heartbreak will savor the cut and thrust of this battle."
    —*Library Journal*

PENGUIN BOOKS

QUEEN B

Juno Dawson is the #1 *Sunday Times* bestselling novelist, screenwriter, journalist, and columnist for *Attitude* magazine. Juno's books include *Her Majesty's Royal Coven* and *The Shadow Cabinet*, as well as the global bestsellers *This Book Is Gay* and *Clean*. She also writes for television and created the official Doctor Who audio drama *Doctor Who: Redacted*. An occasional actress and model, Juno appeared in the BBC's *I May Destroy You* (2020). *Queen B* is a standalone novel within the HMRC universe. She lives in Brighton, UK, with her husband and Chihuahua.

JUNO DAWSON

QUEEN B

✥ THE STORY OF ✥
ANNE BOLEYN,
WITCH QUEEN

PENGUIN BOOKS

PENGUIN BOOKS

An imprint of Penguin Random House LLC
penguinrandomhouse.com

LIBRARY OF CONGRESS CATALOGING-IN-PUBLICATION DATA
Names: Dawson, Juno, author.
Title: Queen B : the story of Anne Boleyn, witch queen / Juno Dawson.
Description: New York : Penguin Books, 2024.
Identifiers: LCCN 2024006232 (print) | LCCN 2024006233 (ebook) |
ISBN 9780143138341 (paperback) | ISBN 9780593512418 (ebook)
Subjects: LCSH: Anne Boleyn, Queen, consort of Henry VIII, King of
England, 1507–1536—Fiction. | Witches—Fiction. | LCGFT:
Witch fiction. | Fantasy fiction. | Novels.
Classification: LCC PR6104.A8868 Q44 2024 (print) | LCC PR6104.
A8868 (ebook) | DDC 823/.92—dc23/eng/20240306
LC record available at https://lccn.loc.gov/2024006232
LC ebook record available at https://lccn.loc.gov/2024006233

Printed in the United States of America
1st Printing

Set in CompatilTextLTPro
Designed by Sabrina Bowers

To Kim,
the most loyal queen

Le temps viendra

Je anne boleyn

The time will come

I Anne Boleyn

—INSCRIPTION WITHIN BOLEYN'S
PERSONAL PRAYER BOOK, LATE 1520S

Maybe I do. Would it be so terrible?

—LADY GAGA, WHEN ASKED IF SHE HAD
A PENIS ON *60 MINUTES*, 2011

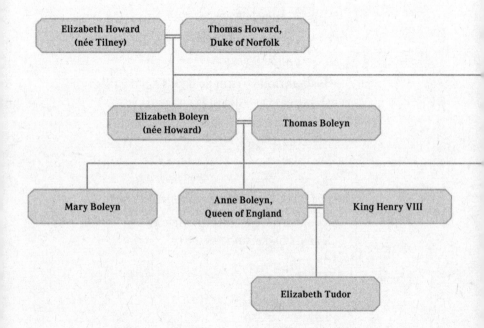

THE HOUSE OF HOWARD
1536

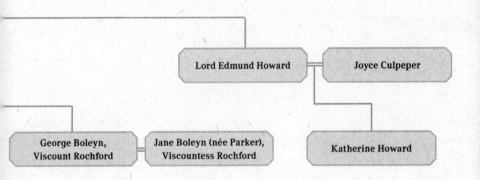

THE COURT OF KING HENRY VIII
1536

Queen Anne Boleyn – *second wife of King Henry VIII*

Princess Elizabeth – *daughter of King Henry VIII and Anne Boleyn*

Lady Jane Boleyn, Viscountess Rochford – *wife of the late George Boleyn, brother to the queen*

Lady Grace Fairfax – *Lady of the Bedchamber*

Lady Cecilia de la Torre – *Lady of the Bedchamber*

Lady Margery de Leon – *costumier to the queen*

Lady Temperance Wycliffe – *Lady of the Bedchamber*

Sir Ambrose Fulke – *king's Special Adviser*

Nan Hobbs – *an elderly nursemaid*

Lady Isabel Agard – *Lady of the Bedchamber*

Lady Margaret Pole, Countess of Salisbury – *former lady-in-waiting to Queen Catherine and governess to Princess Mary*

Lady Jane Seymour – *Lady of the Bedchamber*

Lady Margaret (Meg) Douglas – *First Lady of the Bedchamber and niece of Henry VIII*

Katherine Howard – *ward of the Dowager Duchess of Norfolk*

Thomas Cromwell – *Chief Minister to King Henry VIII*

Henry Fitzroy, Duke of Richmond and Somerset – *illegitimate son of Henry VIII and his former mistress, Elizabeth Blount*

DECEASED

Viscount Rochford, George Boleyn – *brother of the queen*

Catherine of Aragon – *first wife of King Henry VIII*

Cardinal Wolsey – *former Chief Adviser to King Henry VIII*

QUEEN
B

A blade falls . . .

$\cdot\ \bigcirc\ \bigcirc\ \bullet\ \bigcirc\ \bigcirc\ \cdot$

LADY GRACE FAIRFAX

The Tower of London

The Tower and the sky were the same hopeless grey. When the moment came, all was quiet. So quiet, in fact, that they could hear the head hit the wooden platform they'd erected on the green. *Thud.* It bounced once, and rolled once. Appalling, and undignified.

No provision had been made for her burial. She had been a problem to be solved, and now it was done. No man had prepared for the immediate next, and so it fell to the women.

For now, it was enough to get her away from the watchful ghouls at the scaffold on the centre of the courtyard. The ladies-in-waiting took the head and body into the chapel and wept. Their vulgar display was quite ghastly, and the men left. Just as the women had known they would.

Only six witches remained in their coven.

For weeks, they had been detained in the royal lodgings,

sharing in the queen's isolation. It had not been hard to convince Cromwell to allow them to share these final weeks in captivity with the queen; they'd scarcely needed magic. A man preoccupied with self-preservation above all else.

And so they had attended her until the very end. It was their duty, but more than that, they loved her. Clothed in black and grey, they had marched the final procession to the gallows.

Struggling to keep her stiffening limbs aloft, the women now lay the queen's body to rest on the floor before the altar. It was day; the candles were not yet lit. Absurd and unsure, Lady Grace Fairfax cradled the head as a babe. As the others looked to her, she placed it next to the exposed collar. Eyes closed and lips parted, she didn't look like Anne at all; so slack and unrefined. She didn't look *at peace*, she looked *dead*, some wet trout at a fishmonger. Grace tugged the white cloth from the altar, a golden cross clattering to the floor. She placed it over her face.

The women drew close, formed a circle around the body. Now, a dreadful quiet.

Grace looked to her fellow witches. Why was no one doing anything? 'Well?' she said impatiently. 'Revive her.'

The viscountess, Lady Rochford, clasped the silk blindfold to her breast, her knuckles white. 'Heresy, sister. We cannot.'

Grace ignored the outburst, instead turning to the old woman, the healer. 'Nan, can it be done?'

Nan Hobbs dutifully held her papery hands over the body. After a moment, she shook her head. 'There is nothing to heal, child.'

'She is the *queen*,' Grace spat. Sour bile burned under her breastbone. She knew this coarse conduct was beneath her, but how could someone of Anne's magnitude be gone with such scant ceremony? After days of torturous waiting, and weeks of slow decline, it had taken a casual second.

Lady Jane Rochford, now, Grace supposed, their de facto leader, passed through what thin daylight filtered through the stained-glass windows of St Peter ad Vincula. She sighed. 'She is queen no longer. Seymour's girl will be upon the throne by week's end.'

'No queen of mine,' Lady Margery breathed, crouching at Grace's side.

'Nor mine,' agreed Grace.

There followed yet more silence. The air in the church felt oddly relaxed, and Grace found it disrespectful. The nerve of the world, turning when hers had stopped still. The column of meek sunlight advanced across the slabs. In these turgid minutes, Grace reckoned with the truth. Anne was gone, and no witch would bring her back. She was a fool unmasked, because she had not allowed herself to believe it, not truly. How she had courted some divine intervention, if not from the king, from the Mother. She'd have entertained, in her darkest moments, the treacherous tongue of Satanis himself.

And guilt. Such guilt. She could have stopped the blade. Any of them could have. Anne could have, instead of reading her carefully rehearsed lines so dutifully. She could have made the executioner plunge his blade into his own chest. They could have shown the world, at last, what it really was to be a witch. Alas, a display of their nature would bring a rain of fire down upon all witchkind. That, or they were cowards. Grace felt the air around her skin fizz. It was tempting to turn this fury outwards, but for what? *She* could have saved her. She had not.

The church door whined open, breaking her from her stupor. Isabel and Temperance, returning from the White Tower, carrying between them a plain wooden box. 'What is this? Where is the coffin?' Jane said, her face still ashen.

Grace did not much care for the viscountess, but she had not yet seen the woman weep, and she respected her grim resolve in the face of this grinding misery. She looked weary, her eyes sunken and cheeks hollow. Her husband *and* her sister-in-law, gone both, in a matter of hours. Their swift downfall was just that, a terrible fall, a plunge. Perhaps Jane's grief was yet to catch her up. Grace knew a dark tide would engulf her eventually. This was only the start.

'My lady, there is no coffin,' Temperance said, unable to meet her gaze.

'What?' Grace blinked in disbelief.

'This was as good as we could find,' Isabel, the youngest in their coven, said as they set down the grimy arrow box.

'They mock us,' Grace snarled. 'Killing her wasn't enough. Now they defile her.' She looked to the sky beyond the windows, feeling her eyes turn black. She summoned howling westerly winds. Grey clouds, irate, pooled around the Tower.

This day, this city, would mourn Anne Boleyn. They would hear the Mother scream in righteous fury.

Lightning lit the chapel, soon followed by a doleful rumble of thunder.

Jane Rochford clamped a hand on her shoulder. 'Lady Fairfax, I implore you. Reserve your vengeance. You shall require every last drop for the traitor.'

Indeed. There was only one cure for a witch who betrays her coven, and it was purifying fire. Grace Fairfax would find the witch that forsook their gracious queen, their high priestess, her Anne, and she would eviscerate her.

She would avenge the woman she loved with blood.

. . . and a story begins

TEN YEARS EARLIER – SUMMER 1526

○○●○○

LADY GRACE FAIRFAX

Palace of Placentia - London

ourt was new, and loud, and crowded. Who would have believed there were so many people in the world. If the king's empire was a living, breathing beast, Grace found herself in its beating heart. The palace was beyond anything Grace could have imagined; a city within a city. The kitchens alone were greater than her childhood home. She had travelled many furlongs from the swooning moorlands of Yorkshire.

A steady metallic clank echoed from the armoury, a choke of smelt and ore billowing across the yard. Through this smog, a procession of fine horses was led towards the stables. A satisfied Grace waited for them to pass and proceeded with haste, carrying a basket of plums, pomegranates and apples across the servant's yard to the kitchens to be prepared. The queen had demanded her fruits, and Grace was keen to make a good impression. Still not quite sure of the correct order of things, she'd used some initiative and sent a boy to market at once, then loitered at the kitchen gate until his return, wanting Her Majesty to know she had personally secured this bounty.

That was how court worked, her dear aunt Elinor had told her. Be seen; make friends, but only important ones. Avoid gossip, however delicious. Avoid men altogether. So far these rules were working, although she'd only been here a week or so. In that time, she'd only interacted directly with Queen Catherine a handful of times, as was to be expected so soon into her posting, but Grace found her affable and kind, if . . . predisposed. The queen was pious and serious, certainly, devoting many of her waking hours to silent prayer. Grace wanted to ingratiate herself as quickly as she could. She would not risk being sent away. There would be no return.

Outside the palace, the mighty sails of the king's ships on the river caught the milky afternoon sunlight, almost winking. Grace marvelled. The Thames snaked alongside the palace, the river was as wide as any water she'd ever seen. Grace imagined how it would feel one day to see the sea. She felt a very long way away from home, from her husband. She was *free*.

This was all borne of luck, and Grace thanked the blue of the sky. The king was paranoid, still mindful of the north. He was right to be, in her opinion, not that anyone had ever sought that. He wanted the great northern Yorkshire hound obedient and servile, and so the nobles and landowners of the county had to be buttered – men like her husband. Robert Fairfax was a wealthy man. Many years earlier, he had inherited five hundred acres outside Bradford. It was prime grazing land for sheep, their fleeces bound for the county's mills, making him one of the most prosperous men in the north. In the king's eyes he could be a valued ally or an influential dissenter. As such, he'd been bestowed with the title of Lord Fairfax immediately after the war. That was how she, a mere printer's daughter, had become a *lady*.

It was no secret the king liked decorating his court with pretty girls. Among the lords, there was brisk competition as to whose wives attended court regularly. It was a medal of honour: the closer one got to the king or queen, the greater the brag. It was also said the king didn't want too many of the queen's native Spaniards around her, lest they somehow ferret secrets back to the king of Spain. It hadn't, therefore, been at all difficult for Lord Fairfax to install Grace, young, pretty and very English, in London.

Grace had tried to hide her delight, she really had. She had dutifully dabbed imaginary tears from her eyes while edging towards the carriage, just as Robert had made the appropriate overtures about how the hall wouldn't be the same without her. Neither had acknowledged the young scullery maid or her swollen belly.

She had been nervous, of course. She had never been to the other side of the Pennines her entire life – but this opportunity would rid her of Robert. Finally.

And so she would be the best lady-in-waiting the queen had

ever had. For one thing, she was wholly immune to the famished stares of the king. He had *noticed* Grace the first time she attended church with Catherine, and she had noticed him noticing her. All her life, people had remarked at Grace's beauty: her alabaster skin, her almost-white hair. It was remarkable, she supposed, in that people oft remarked on it. But no one did *cold* quite like Grace Fairfax. As the king had sized her up, she'd brought an icy chill about his neck.

That was something she could do. Since she was a child, Grace could make things happen just by thinking of them.

No sooner had the king eyed her than he'd recoiled. All he could think about was getting away from her.

She was mulling on this first encounter with the king when she fell. As she took a step up to enter the Boiling Kitchen, she tripped over her hem. Her only thought was to protect the fruit, and she wrapped her body around it as she tumbled. Instinctively, she summoned a little air around herself to cushion the fall. She landed on her knees, a couple of plums rolling across the flagstones. Her knees hurt, although not as badly as her pride.

'Here, allow me,' a kind voice said, and a girl appeared at her side, stooping to pick up the plums. Grace recognised her as another of Catherine's ladies.

So far, Grace had sensed the other ladies evaluating her, trying to establish if she was some sort of a threat. To *whom* she couldn't fathom. She'd been at court only eight days, and already she sensed something amiss. It seemed the queen was not in favour with the king. There was much to learn.

'Are you hurt?' the girl asked as they made their way past the network of larders and salting rooms towards the kitchen.

'I aren't,' Grace said.

'I *aaaren't!*' the girl imitated her long Yorkshire vowels. 'I just love your accent. It's so funny.'

Grace felt her face warm. She was, of course, aware that people of the south sounded different to those in the north, but she hadn't been prepared for just how much she'd stand out. Already, she found herself trying to copy the rounded vowels of the elite.

The Spanish girl was becoming, a sprinkle of freckles across her cherub nose, and her hair escaping her bonnet in tight auburn ringlets. She placed the fruit back in the basket. 'Are these for Her Majesty?'

'Yes.' Grace had a creeping sense that the younger, yet more experienced, girl was about to relieve her of her haul.

'Wonderful, I was sent to fetch her a posset. We can go together.' She smiled and looped her arm through Grace's. 'I'm Cecilia. Lady de la Torre.'

'Lady Fairfax. Grace.'

'I know who you are. We've spoken of little else all week.' Cecilia grinned naughtily as they entered the thrum of the Great Kitchen. The air was delicious, thick with hog fat. A turnbroach stood at the spit, dutifully turning the roast over the flames. 'That's not true, but a newcomer is always an event. Especially a pretty one . . .'

Grace silently cursed the shape of her face. In truth, it had brought her nothing but trouble. She'd been betrothed to Robert at thirteen, married at fourteen, having been classed *eligible* when she was nine or ten. She had two eyes, a nose and a mouth like anyone else; it was perplexing.

Fending off the compliment, Grace instead asked, 'Why? Because of Lady Blount?' *That* scandal was no currency; Grace had briefly met the little lord, the king's bastard, just yesterday.

A couple of the kitchen girls giggled at the mention of the mistress's name. Cecilia fixed them with a look and they scuttled back to their duties. 'Keep your voice down! We just call her Bessie around here, but no, she's long since gone.' She then added conspiratorially, 'But what do you make of Lady Boleyn?'

This was not the first time she'd heard the name Anne Boleyn. She was only one of the queen's ladies, but everyone seemed especially keen to find favour with her. Maybe that meant something. 'I think nothing of her; we haven't met. Why? Is she favoured by the queen?'

Even the flustered cook rolled her eyes a little at her naivety. Cecilia laughed unreservedly as Cook handed her a fresh posset. 'Dear sweet Grace, you have much to learn! Come let's take these to the waning queen.'

'You watch your mouth Mistress Cecilia!' Cook slapped Cecilia on the rear as they departed, and she hooted once more.

'So Lady Fairfax,' Cecilia asked as they crossed the sunny courtyard in the direction of the queen's apartments. 'Where does Lord Fairfax reside?'

'To the north. In Yorkshire.'

'I see. Do you miss him terribly?'

'Oh yes, very much so,' Grace lied.

Cecilia laughed gaily, although Grace wasn't sure why. Nonetheless, Grace had made her first friend. She wasn't yet sure if she had made an important one.

Some days later, Grace awoke to a voice inside her head.

Grace Fairfax, hear me.

Grace sat up in her cot and looked around the bedchamber. In the next bed, Cecilia slept soundly. They had been assigned to share a chamber shortly after they had met that day in the kitchen. She was about to dismiss the strange premonition as a dream when she heard it again. The words filled her skull, clear and precise.

Lady Fairfax, hear me. Come to the wine cellar. Come at once. Tell no one.

A swift fever swept over her, and Grace almost vomited. Her hand flew to her mouth. One of *them*. In *court*. It had been many, many years since she'd heard another speak to her in this manner. Her aunt Elinor, back in Bingley, had taught her about their kind when she was a little girl, and what they could do. She had also stressed, in the sternest possible terms, that she must conceal her gifts, whatever the cost. She must never use *that* word to describe herself. Should not utter it aloud, not ever. Not even her mother and father knew what she was capable of, both rather more concerned with marrying off their bonnie daughters than truly seeing them.

Grace had been so, so careful. No one down here knew what she was. *She* scarcely knew what she was. This southern witch must be an enchantress, able to delve amongst her thoughts. She felt suddenly cornered, a hare in a trap.

She tried to calm herself with the salve of reason: Whoever spoke to her thusly was abnormal too, and that meant they were at an equal disadvantage. Another like her, this far south; Grace could scarcely believe it.

The voice called again.

Make haste. Come to the cellar. You won't be seen or heard. Be assured the palace sleeps. You and I are the only souls awake.

Grace rose from her bed and threw a cape over her chemise. Barefoot, so as to make less noise, Grace tiptoed through the palace. The mysterious siren was true to her word; everyone slept, spellbound. Even the guard posted outside the queen's bedchamber snored, chin to his chest.

She had never seen these halls so tranquil. Grace found she liked this midnight kingdom, her own private palace. She carried herself more lightly, ran her fingers over the brocade curtains, felt the rugs between her toes. Down staircases and hallways Grace went, intuitively finding her way to the cellars off the kitchens. Embers still glowed in the great hearth.

Thinking ahead, she plucked a stubby candle from the mantel and lit the wick with her powers. Grace did not work well with fire, but a little she could muster safely. Holding it afront her, she traversed the narrow alleyway from the kitchen to the main cellars, the cobblestones cold on her bare feet. The Sergeant of the Cellar too was asleep at his post. Grace slipped past him and down the stairs into the cellars.

As she descended, the air grew musty, earthen. Her heart thumped in her chest. If she had to, she'd fight. She'd kept herself a secret this long.

Reaching the bottom of the stone steps, Grace surveyed the cellar. There were rows and rows of barrels of mead, wine and ale. In the middle of it all, another candle flickered amidst the blackest darkness, a lone jewel. 'Show yourself,' Grace whispered to the figure waiting in the shadows.

A caped woman stepped forward, peeling back her velvet cowl. She held the candle close to her chin. 'There's no need to whisper,' Lady Anne Boleyn said, eyes almost golden in the flame.

'*You*,' Grace breathed, and instantly regretted it.

'Me,' Boleyn said, a faint smile on her lips. She was a striking woman, about the same age as Grace – twenty years or thereabouts – with high cheekbones and full lips. Her chestnut hair tumbled out from under her hood, almost to her waist. Seemingly at home, she crossed the cellar floor, goblet in hand. She helped herself to a generous glug. 'Port? I enjoy a port at this hour.'

'I shan't,' Grace said. 'How did you do that? Summon me so?'

Boleyn looked almost disappointed, a tilt of her head. 'Come now, Lady Fairfax, let us not play coy with one another. I knew what *you* were the second you made your debut. You ought to know exactly how.'

It made a sort of sense. Grace had only seen Boleyn from afar, but she was never alone. Women, men, boys and girls, they all flocked to her it seemed. Little worker bees tending to their hive queen. Enchanting indeed. Even so, Grace wasn't about to admit to anything with a perfect stranger, enchantress or not. She said nothing.

'Of course, I had Cecilia confirm my suspicions.' When Grace remained silent, Boleyn went on. 'Grace, if I may, you have nothing to fear. We are witches both.'

Grace flinched at the word. Boleyn considered her with hooded eyes, as if she was evaluating her inside and out. It was greatly disconcerting, and Grace folded her arms like a breastplate across her chest. 'How sad,' Boleyn said. 'You are so ashamed. Why?'

'I'm no witch, I didn't choose this. I can't help it.'

Boleyn smiled. 'It's not a slur, Grace, far from it. A witch is a powerful, natural thing. Would you recoil so from a mighty oak or while gazing up at a proud mountain?'

'No,' Grace admitted.

'It is all one thing. We are part of Mother's great design. We were bestowed with our gifts for a reason. Her reason. If they want to fear the witch, that's a problem for man. Let them fear the wind.'

Grace felt naked, exposed and foolish. All that hiding, and for what? They'd seen her for what she was in seconds. 'And what of Lady de la Torre?'

'Cecilia is like us. And Lady Jane, and others.' Lady Rochford? That was a shock; she was so dour.

'All of them?'

'Of the ladies-in-waiting? No, of course not. To be as we are is rare indeed. But like attracts like.' Boleyn came closer. Every time Grace dared to look into her face, she found the other woman's eyes ready for her. She didn't look away once, reeling her in. 'There are five of us now. We are a coven. A court coven, if you can believe such a thing. We first came together during our time in France, and then travelled here as one. Come, let us sit by the fire.'

As Anne led her back towards the kitchen, Grace was dying to ask *why*, but there was a more pertinent question. 'Does the queen know?'

'Ha! Of course not! And nor does the king, before you ask. Tell me, Lady Fairfax, are you pledged to a coven in the north?'

Grace shook her head. 'My husband isn't aware of what I am. I have . . . I have never belonged to a coven.'

Boleyn gave her arm a supportive squeeze as she pulled a maid's stool to the hearthside and beckoned her to sit. 'I am sorry to hear that, but confess a certain satisfaction because it means you are free to join ours?' she said hopefully. 'A witch without her coven is only half a thing. I sense great power in you, Grace. You are a bright light.'

Unused to such hyperbole, Grace looked to the floor, bashful. She could feel the warmth of the embers on her face and hoped Boleyn wouldn't catch her flustering. There was something about this woman. Physically, she was pale and slight, not especially tall, but seemed to tower over the room, some titan. To come here alone by dead of night, to use her gift so expansively, took gall. If either of them wielded *great power*, it was her.

'You're a sorceress?' Boleyn prompted.

'I am, my lady.' Grace knew enough from what Aunt Elinor had told her. Not all witches were alike. Some could read minds; move objects through thought alone. Others could heal the sick. Some saw premonitions of what was to come, and sorceresses – like Grace – could master the elements. At least, Grace could master *most* of them.

'Call me Anne, I beg,' she said. 'All those names and titles and rules are for court. Here we are free from that exhausting codework. Free to be women, and witches, and friends.'

'Very well. Then I am Grace.'

Another dazzling smile. 'Aren't you just! We don't have a sorceress among us at present, so you'd be doing us a great favour by sharing your skill. Do say you'll join us, Grace? We meet in the King's Chapel at midnight, just once or twice a week. No one shall ever know; I'll make certain of it.' She tapped her head with a finger.

Grace considered her offer. She had escaped here to be free of Robert, not to rediscover her strange heritage, but this felt proper somehow. Her aunt, the only other person with this affliction Grace had known, had schooled her to believe that there was a Great Mother who birthed the world, and she saw everything in eternity. Grace couldn't help but wonder if this was foreplanned. Where was the harm? 'Yes,' she said. 'Yes, I shall.'

Anne smiled broadly. 'I know what you're thinking,' she said. 'And I quite agree. You coming here, your arrival at court in this precise moment, is a path ordained by the Mother. You *belong* here. You belong here with us.' She took her hand and gave it a companionable squeeze. 'And with me.'

The door to the kitchen opened with a scrape, and Grace quickly withdrew her hand. Her first instinct was to flee and, from the ashes, an angry flame lashed at them – she couldn't control it. Anne flinched from the fire, ruffled at last. 'Peace, sister. We're safe.'

Cecilia de la Torre slunk through the dark gap in the kitchen door, stopped when she saw them together. She bowed her head slightly, deferring to Anne. 'Ah, I see you told her.'

'Sister. Welcome Grace to the coven . . . '

And now, the fugitive . . .

LADY CECILIA DE LA TORRE

Bisham Manor - Berkshire

The mare, a rust hobby she'd taken from court, thundered towards the manor house. Hooves pummelled wet clay. Cecilia gripped the reins tighter, hands pink and raw, struggling to see. The rain fell as rods, shifting side to side, as a curtain would. The work of the witches, Cecilia had no doubt. As the queen had breathed her last, the sky had gone furiously dark. A sorceress, likely Grace.

She had never seen the true extent of Grace Fairfax and it scared her.

Arriving at Bisham after nightfall, she secured the horse first. The stable boy was perhaps a little surprised to see such a bedraggled creature arrive so late, but he recovered his wits and agreed to show her to the house.

She entered through the tradesmen's entrance, shivering from both the rain and sheer mania. Her hair had fallen loose, hanging as wet frizz down her neck. What a forlorn figure she must be. A servant took her cape, while another went to alert the countess. Cecilia gratefully accepted a posset, her hands shaking, as she was led to the fireplace in the Great Hall.

It was a message. By putting her in such a formal room, Cecilia understood she wasn't wholly welcome here. The tapestries that adorned the walls were dark, foreboding, depicting the hunts. A stag, wild-eyed with fear, looked to her for mercy.

'Why would you presume to darken my door?' the countess's voice boomed as she swept into the hall, her maids at her hems.

Cecilia said nothing, staring into the hearth. She was no seer, but she saw her future in the flames.

'Leave us,' Lady Margaret told her girls. 'Now.' Her staff sank back into the manor, and they were left alone. Cecilia felt annoyance radiate from the woman in humid orange pulses. 'Well? Explain yourself. Do you have the faintest idea how precarious my position is, Cecilia? Cromwell watches my every move. Like spiders, he has spies in every crevice.'

Cecilia looked to her. The fates of the Pole clan were prized gossip at court; her predicament wasn't news to Cecilia. 'I heard the rumours about your son.'

Lady Margaret sighed deeply. The woman had aged: a permanent fret carved her forehead, and her hair was more silver than black. Troublesome years had taken their toll. 'They aren't rumours. Reginald, fool he is, has made great noise of his allegiance to Rome,' she admitted. 'He may as well have painted a target on his back. And mine.'

'And what of you?' Cecilia dared ask in the privacy of the hall.

'I am loyal to our beloved and benevolent king,' Margaret said flatly, as if hexed. 'I wrote to my son telling him as much.'

Cecilia understood the countess's quandary. The king had taken it upon himself to rewrite the rules of Heaven, and now Catholicism was treason. Truly, what sort of a mad king takes on God? She nodded and sipped the foam off her drink. The sack was warm, almost sickly sweet. Cecilia's hands wouldn't cease their trembling.

Margaret – another enchantress – softened, no doubt sensing her fear. 'You can understand, child, that I do not wish to draw yet more eyes to my house,' she said. 'You must leave this place at once.'

'Please! I need your help!' Cecilia blurted out. 'They'll be coming for me.'

Lady Margaret didn't need to ask who. She nodded and smoothed down her skirts to sit opposite her. A chess set sat between them, mid-play. Here, at least, the queen was protected. 'So it's true?' Margaret breathed, flames dancing in her pale eyes. 'It was *you*?'

'Is it known?' Cecilia fought to keep her tone even. She was scared. More scared than she'd ever been. Tired, too: the *weeks* she'd spent in the lodgings at the Tower with the queen and the others, shielding her thoughts all through the endless days and nights, had taken a toll. She craved sleep. She was close to welcoming Death himself for the respite.

Lady Margaret sighed. 'Child, Anne Boleyn was no fool. There are a finite number of us who know the truth. It was plain: someone in the coven betrayed her. Your presence here suggests you're our little Judas, or instead you worry they *think* it was you. So which is it?'

Cecilia felt the fire kiss her cheeks and thought how it would feel, the burning. Would it hurt? Would she feel the skin crack and peel back off her skull? For how *long* would she feel it? She said nothing. Lady Margaret wouldn't understand her reasons, and Cecilia had some secrets even the countess didn't know. She intended them to remain private.

'It *was* you.' Lady Margaret's eyes were cold, steely, even with fire in them. 'Why would you do such a thing? Moreover, why would you bring your stink here to my home?' The countess's face grew even more stony.

'To whom else could I turn?'

She laughed ruefully. 'You surely have favour with the king if no one else. He got what he wanted, after all. Is that what this is, child, are your sights set on the throne?'

'No!' she protested. 'I'd sooner die.'

'Fortuitous, I'd say.'

Cecilia chose to ignore her glib tongue. She'd never especially liked the countess, she was far from maternal, but she had served Queen Catherine well and had taken Cecilia under her tutelage when she'd first arrived in England. 'I need passage to Padua.'

'And why would I help?'

'Because I am Catholic.'

Lady Margaret now laughed heartily. 'Child, I think we both know that isn't true.'

'You condemn yourself,' retorted Cecilia. She knew some of the countess's secrets too. She'd be sure to remind her. 'Witch.'

'I am a *witch* by birth and a Catholic by *choice*. I received the Lord and absolved myself of sin.' All those hours the countess spent on her knees praying to be cured of her nature. Cecilia found it perverse. Lady Margaret went on. 'You abandoned righteousness the second you joined the queen's coven. You pledged an oath did you not, child?'

Cecilia wished she'd stop calling her a child. She was not a girl. Growing up in her cruel uncle's home had forced her out of girlhood. Unable to remember her native Aragón, Cecilia had lost both her parents to the flu of 1512. She'd been less than a year old and given over to her aunt and uncle in Tripoli. At the first opportunity, a day into thirteen, she'd fled to England to serve in the court of Queen Catherine. Her aunt had been glad to be rid of her, and Cecilia was finally free of her uncle's attention.

Still, she was unwed and without child, so in the eyes of the world, a *girl* she would remain.

She took Margaret Pole's hands in hers. 'Please, I beg of you. Your son never supported Anne, or her union with the king. I thought you of all people would understand. Could you write to Reginald again, arrange safe passage? He could hasten me away to a convent.'

Margaret seemed to consider her plea a moment. 'No, I think not. It would be unwise to make an enemy of the coven. If nothing else, the queen achieved a considerable arsenal.'

A fresh jolt of panic gripped her guts. The things Cecilia had seen. The fateful night on the bank of the Thames haunted her still. She knew *exactly* what the coven was capable of.

Lady Margaret went to leave, but Cecilia clutched her sleeve. 'Stop!' she said, desperate. 'It would be less wise still to make an enemy of the king, would it not? Cromwell thinks he found a witch. Do you think he'll stop at one? She was the start of things to come. *Any* woman who displeases them will find herself a witch whether she is one or not. My lady, I have Cromwell's ear . . . '

That wasn't strictest truth, but it mattered not. As the countess glared down at her, Cecilia saw the faintest glint of fear in her eyes, and she knew she'd won.

LADY GRACE FAIRFAX

Bermondsey - London

Grace sniffed at her pomander, trying to mask the putrid smell of the poor. Did the king know people lived in such squalor? Did he not care? They were a long way from court, but he had eyes everywhere. These streets were no place for a lady but, fortunately, these ladies were also witches. Jane and Margery, enchantresses both, shielded them from onlookers as they moved amongst the lowliest hovels of Bermondsey.

'It's this way,' Margery said, her tight black curls emerging from under her cowl like a halo.

'Can you feel them?' Grace asked.

'We're close.'

Even at this unseemly hour, even in the dire weather, the Shambles were jammed with filthy children, beggars, whores, dogs and rats. Ramshackle timber-frame buildings seemed to constrict around them, the streets growing narrower as they neared the river. Brown water gushed along the gutters, and Grace was careful of where she planted her feet. Not seeing the four women in velvet capes, a drunk staggered past them, heading in the direction of the almshouse.

'Where are their parents?' Temperance, not much more than a girl herself, surveyed one waif, hands out inside a doorway. 'How do they survive?'

'Most do not,' Jane said sadly.

'Couldn't we come back on the morrow? In the light?' Temperance asked with trepidation.

Grace strode onwards. 'It must be now.' She wanted the traitor *tonight*. With every passing minute she put distance between them. Moreover, if they retired now, Grace feared she might never get up again. That she would lay back and let a tide of pain wash her out to sea.

The four of them had come to this slum directly from the Tower estate. Grace herself had torn a deep chunk out of the floor of St Peter ad Vincula to make space for their queen. She was returned to the earth, part of the Mother once more. Through the soil and the air and the water, Anne would live forever.

Grace turned her face to the rain, and searched for any trace of her now; anything would do, any meaningless sign to find comfort in. She felt nothing, only numbness. She wanted to scream, but bit her lip. The notion that she was *at rest* made her flesh crawl. Anne did not rest. She hadn't rested a day of her life.

'This is it,' Margery said, turning down a narrow alleyway. 'The washerwomen's shop.'

'Are you certain?' Jane said, eyeing the darkened passage that ran alongside the structure. The building seemed to lean drunkenly, harassing the next. Grace knew precisely where they were but said nothing. Jane had never learned of that accursed night by the river, and it was best to keep it that way.

Margery led the way. Single file, they squeezed down the snicket until Margery descended stone steps to a cellar. 'Margery, caution, I pray,' Temperance said, wide eyes catching what little light there was.

Grace pushed past them both, and removed her glove, ready to strike. 'Let me.'

She hoisted up her skirts and took the lead. At the foot of the stairs, she came to an unlocked door, rotten with damp. She cast a final look at a worried Margery and entered.

The cellar was dark. Her fellow witches waited patiently for her to light the way, but Grace stalled.

Grace had never been a fire witch. Even as a sorceress, and a powerful one at that, she was far more attuned to the air, to water. She could summon flame, naturally, but found it hard to control. Fire was wilful, hungry. It sought only to consume. In truth, Grace was scared of it. Once, as a girl, she'd set alight a derelict barn while still discovering her gifts. She'd been alone on a dusty July afternoon, trying to learn what she could do if she concentrated. She still remembered how the tiny flame she bore galloped away from her, spread and devoured the dry timber. She'd been powerless to stop it.

Now she became aware of Jane's judgement, a faint huff. A sorceress who couldn't master fire. Shameful. Temperance came alongside her, a polite ball of fire swimming in her palm. Grace nodded gratefully, though envious of the younger witch's mastery.

She now saw the ceiling to the cellar was held aloft by worn beams in the centre of the room, while to the sides there were shelves of clean linens, ready for collection. Away from the street, the odour improved, but the scuttling, snuffling and squeaking of rats grew noisier. She hoped Margery might steer them away. Other than the vermin, the cellar appeared empty.

'Where are they?' Temperance breathed, casting her flame around the room.

The answer came from below. There was a rustle, close by. At first, she thought it a rat, but from aside Grace's foot, a dead, festering hand burst up through the matted dirt and straw. Grace recoiled, colliding with Margery. The floor ruptured, and an emaciated arm soon followed the hand, hoisting a diseased form out of the earth. The figure, possibly male, dragged itself towards her. His skin was wet, oozing with yellow pus, and the noxious stink of pestilence. Behind her, Temperance screamed. Grace retreated further.

Margery seized her arm as another carcass crawled up out of the dirt. Regaining composure, Grace fought. She pulled the night air into her skin, leeching its innate power. From somewhere deep in her bones, Grace massaged the giddy sensation to and fro, feeling it build and build within. To her, this was second nature, and took mere seconds. When she felt fit to burst, she directed the tingling sensation down her arms to her hands and let it all out. She unleashed whiplash bolts of pure lightning at the first plagued corpse. The entire cellar was exposed in blinding white light, but it made no difference. It continued to lunge at them, blackened nails outstretched. It made a sickening guttural moan, as if its tongue had been cut off. The smell, oh, the smell was fetid.

More diseased figures, all poxed, covered in weeping sores and pustules, lumbered out of the dankest shadows.

Suddenly, Jane pushed past Grace and held aloft both hands. 'This isn't real,' she announced. 'It's a phantasm. See as I see.'

Grace screwed her eyes shut and felt Jane's sight impose itself. There was nothing before them. When she opened her eyes again, the apparitions were gone. She stiffened. How? It had felt – *smelt* – so real. The witches of Bermondsey were stronger than she'd ever granted them. She gathered herself again, ready to fight for real.

Jane stepped further into the darkness. 'Sisters, show yourselves, I demand it.'

There followed another movement of rat feet, until an archway appeared in the rear wall. Grace cursed herself, more than a little embarrassed. She should have recognised the illusion. She wrapped her hands in light, poised to strike. Sparks licked her arms, snapped on her skin.

A familiar, ruddy face stepped out of the shadows first. She wore a white cloth cap over her hair and a shrewd expression. Despite their dank surroundings, her apron and face were spotless, and she wore polished boots on her feet: a proud woman. She was soon followed by a tall, rotund witch who loomed over her companion, some sort of sentry. Grace vowed not to get too close. More witches followed, their woollen clothes in various states of disarray, carrying candles or lanterns. Soon, the ladies of court were vastly outnumbered. Grace wondered if their excursion had been foolhardy. These women would not be welcomed in court; it was perhaps arrogance to assume the opposite was true.

Alas, they had something they needed.

The first woman spoke. 'Well, looky looky, girls. We got a viscountess in the laundry. Who'd have thought it!' She scowled at Jane before turning to her acolytes. 'What are you waiting for? They're ladies! Curtsy, you cunts!'

The women and girls sniggered as they made a great display of bowing to them. Grace sighed, frustrated. This was wasting precious time. Cecilia could cover a lot of ground while they were playing games.

Jane rose above the mockery, politely bowing in return. 'Agnes. I trust my raven found her way to you? It's been a long time.'

Agnes considered her rival. 'Ten years to be exact, my lady. I remember because it was the spring of '26 when you had me removed from the kitchens at Grimston.'

Grace looked to Jane now, unaware she too had a personal history with Agnes Drury. Jane blushed. 'Regrettable. As I explained at the time, my husband—'

Agnes smiled; her teeth black and broken. 'And how is Viscount Rochford?' The witches behind her stifled laughter.

Jane did not flinch. 'My husband is dead.'

Agnes shook her head. 'I jest, you daft cunt. Sorry about George. It true he fucked his sister?'

Grace lit up with lightning, ready to unleash her glory on the witch. Maybe she ought to have killed her the last time they met.

'Grace, stop!' Jane barked, and Grace found she couldn't take another step forward.

'Ooh, the feisty one!' Agnes grinned. 'I remember you from our night by the river . . . '

Grace stood down. She didn't care to remember that night.

Jane released her grip on Grace. It was Jane's turn to be at a disadvantage. 'Of what does she speak?'

Agnes smirked, wordlessly daring Grace to tell the truth. But she would not betray Anne. Not now. And the only *other* person who knew the tale of that night would be dead soon enough. 'It is of no consequence,' Grace lied, occluding her memories. 'I was sent by the queen to consult the seer. Once, last year.'

Jane seemed satisfied with this. 'If you know Lady Fairfax, allow me to introduce Lady Margery De Leon and Lady Temperance Wycliffe.'

Agnes lingered on one, then the other, appraising. 'In that case, I'll be Lady Agnes Drury. What even makes a lady a lady anyway? I got a clef just the same as you do.' The witch almost danced across the floor, performing for them all. 'Where's Old Nan?'

'Back at court. This sad day took its toll.'

'Shame. She's always welcome down here, even if we're not welcome there.'

Jane glowered at Agnes, impatient. 'Agnes, stop. This is lunacy. What would you have me do? You people in court, would be . . .'

Agnes ceased her idling and glared. '*You people?* What people is that, Lady Jane? Whores? Harlots? Bawds? What about mawkins? Paupers? No, m'dear. I think the word you're searchin' for is *witches*. Well, you and I both, love.'

'Precisely,' Grace stepped in, wanting an end to this needless conference. 'We are all witches. Whatever our differences. We are sisters all.'

The witches of Bermondsey loudly disagreed with the sentiment. 'Her Majesty did like to surround herself with pretty little jewels, didn't she?' Agnes's calloused fingers reached for Grace's jaw. 'You are a lovely one, ain't you? But you're a fucking imbecile if you think we're sisters. You're only here cos you wants something.'

Grace marvelled at Agnes's stupidity. Could she be so blind? 'Of course we do! We must find the traitor at once. She was willing to betray her queen. Do you think the same fate won't befall the rest of us?'

Agnes was quieter now. 'We might as well be living in different worlds, and yours is a thousand miles away. You lot in your castles don't even see us. We don't exist to your lords and sirs. Your tittle-tattle at court don't concern us down here.'

'Yes it does!' Grace was shocked to hear her voice so hysterical. Ladies do not caterwaul.

'There is a book,' Jane said, her tone even. 'They call it the *Malleus Maleficarum*.'

'The what now?' Agnes replied, unimpressed.

'The Hammer of Witches,' Grace finished. 'It tells men how to find and kill us.'

'In France they spoke of little else,' said Jane. 'Panic is spreading like a disease. They're printing more and more copies of the infernal book with every passing day, it's an obsession. Things . . . things could go badly for us all.'

'I dare say they'd come for you before us,' Grace finished, and she didn't need to be an enchantress to know Agnes knew it to be true.

Some of the washerwomen whispered amongst themselves, and Grace found herself wishing she *could* hear their thoughts. Agnes seethed. 'This be the queen's fault,' she hissed, silencing the chatter. 'When she came to me winter gone, I told her she was on a path to the gallows, but would she heed my words?' She looked to Grace. 'I warned you too, Pretty.'

'Her Majesty was strong of will,' Grace muttered.

'Oh aye, I remember.'

'And her intentions were sound,' she said more forcefully. 'The best way to ensure our future, our safety, is to take the throne.' Anne's great design: the dawn of an empire of witches.

'And how is that going for Her Majesty?' Agnes sneered, and Grace felt her hot breath on her chin. 'Is his new dolly one of us?'

'No,' Margery interjected. 'Seymour knows nothing of us.'

'What about the Fitzroy bastard?' Jane just shook her head. 'Then you're fucked, ain't you? Your whole great scheme rests in tatters at your satin feet.'

'No,' Jane barked. 'We're still in court. We serve the king and his lords. We have their ears and their minds.'

'And their cocks.' A young witch behind Agnes spoke up. 'That how you serve 'em? With your mouths and cunnies?'

How to argue with that? How tawdry Anne's trajectory must have looked from down here. Bewitch a king, supplant a queen. Even gossipmongers who found the rumours of witchcraft and incest a little far-fetched thought her at the least a craven whore. Grace once more felt her heart shrink and harden. She had watched Anne for so long now, wielding her borrowed power in court, and hiding her true power at all costs. 'When the time comes, we will have *real* power,' Grace said quietly. 'We must have faith, faith in ourselves. We don't need to live this way, fearful and cowering. *That* was the queen's vision. We are stronger than they are.'

They all knew this was true, and for a moment, no one spoke

because it was all so ludicrous, how they hid. They shared that, if nothing else.

'How long will you have us wait down here by the stinking river, swimming in shit?' Agnes said, her bravura slipping. 'When is it our turn? When will the men curtsy to us?'

'Soon,' said Jane, and Grace heard she meant it. 'We had a witch on the throne, don't you see? And we can do so again. *Soon*. My sister, I acknowledge I have slighted you in the past, but now I ask you to trust in me. We are in striking distance of the throne still.'

They shared a meaningful glance, and then Agnes Drury nodded deliberately. Grace did not hear what machinations Jane Rochford planted in Agnes's mind, but she could guess. One way or another, she didn't envisage Lady Seymour, or any fruit she bore, living a long and healthy life.

Agnes seemed to consider whatever future Jane had unfurled before her. 'What is it you want?'

'Where is the seer?'

'Thought as much. *The seer* has a name.' She turned to the giant woman. 'Fetch Sindony.'

She returned a moment later with a very young girl. Grace took care to hide her shock. The girl looked worse still. Sindony was a waiflike thing, and she couldn't be more than eleven or twelve years old, yet she was already entirely bald and walked with a cane. Still, she was also wrapped in a thick fur, and had shoes on her feet. The coven cared for her. She was their greatest treasure.

'She's so young,' Temperance breathed.

'Is she?' Agnes taunted her. Sometimes with witches it was hard to tell. 'And rinse that idea out your head, Jane Rochford, she stays here with us. While we've got Little Sindony, I know we're safe.'

Grace took it back. Agnes wasn't a fool, not a drop. 'Tell me,' Grace asked the girl directly. 'Did you see it? The downfall of the queen?'

The seer said nothing until Agnes granted her permission. 'You can talk to them, doll.'

Sindony took a step closer. 'It was foreseen, my lady. It was always a matter of time. The king is as the storm. He cannot love, cannot reason, only rolls relentlessly forward, destroying all in his path. He will not stop.'

Jane placed a gloved hand on Grace's arm. 'And what of the traitor Cecilia de la Torre?'

'I see fire.'

Grace saw fire in Cecilia's future too.

'A warm hall. A *great* hall. She travelled by land. The countryside. A cross of gold, bejewelled.' The girl giggled. 'The God-fearing witches fear God together.'

Jane looked to Grace. *Margaret Pole.*

◦ ○ ◐ ● ○ ○ ◦

LADY GRACE FAIRFAX

Hampton Court - Middlesex

Capes billowing, the witches cut across the night sky, weaving between each other as they flew. Grace let the air coil itself around her body, suspending her high above London. Up here, the air was sweeter, sharper, and she felt reinvigorated by the moonlight. But when Jane, Temperance and Margery began their descent, she was baffled. *Are we not bound for Bisham?*

Not tonight, Jane told her. Grace tried to argue, but the others continued towards court. They landed on the lawns of the orangery, next to the tiltyard, deserted in the small hours. Somewhere far away, a dog howled, but they were alone. A short flight, and they were a far cry from the squalor they'd just witnessed. Grace saw Jane read the area, confirming their privacy.

Grace's feet touched springy grass, and she drew herself tall. 'What are you doing? We must make haste.'

'No,' Jane said more firmly. 'The child's vision was undeniably useful, but incomplete. We don't know who else is present at Bisham. For all we know Cromwell is there himself and it's a trap meant to lure us in.'

'You think he's protecting Cecilia?' It made sense. Perhaps she'd traded Anne for her own safety. It also wouldn't surprise her if the Lady Margaret had done the same, given the king's fury at her son. That, sadly, was the way of things at court. How to reason with a cobra; you play it a tune.

'I don't know,' Jane admitted. 'Cecilia hid her thoughts well. Who can say what her plans are. But I do know if we storm Bisham Manor, the king will be aware something is afoot if he isn't already.'

She was right, curse her. 'Tomorrow.'

'Tomorrow.' Jane gave Grace's arm a somewhat stiff squeeze, an approximation of a kind gesture. 'I feel your rage, sister, and I match it. She will pay, you have my word. She must not be allowed to threaten all we have worked for.'

Grace nodded, although it was more than a little late for that. How effortlessly Jane had assumed the role of High Priestess. She wondered if some part of her was enjoying this. Jane was no older than the rest of them, and yet she'd always been matronly, not maternal. She and George had no children; a sore subject. If it was not spoken of before his death, it certainly wouldn't be now. Perhaps this coven crusade would give her life shape. Grace had no such clarity.

What of her now?

'I vote we rest,' Jane told them all. 'The days and nights ahead are uncertain.'

An understatement. Grace longed for the days when each dawn didn't bring some terrible twist, some mad whim from the throne room. The baby, Catherine's death, the arrest. Today alone felt to have been a year long. The gentler pastures of 1535 felt like a lifetime ago. To live unafraid would be a luxury.

With that in mind, the witches hurried back to the queen's apartments, on alert for guards. Who could say what permutation court had undergone during the two weeks they'd spent at the Tower. They still, presumably, occupied the rooms close to Anne's bedchamber, although no doubt changes had been made to accommodate Seymour. The thought of returning to her duties, but serving a different queen, hollowed Grace inside. Hopefully the morning would bring renewed vigour.

Grace found her chambers much as she had left them when they went to the Tower. Grace was pleased Seymour hadn't moved into the queen's chambers as yet. That would be in poor taste, she supposed, even for the king. Tomorrow, she would report to Meg, whom she *assumed* was still Mistress of the Bedchamber, and reacquaint herself with court.

Alas, there was one final task Grace had to complete before she could rest her head.

Margery bid her goodnight from the corridor, but Grace caught her hand and waited for Jane and Temperance to vanish into their rooms. 'Wait, sister,' she breathed. 'We are not done yet.'

Margery stood, hands on hips, regarding the painting in the low light of a single candle. Grace only dared light one lest they attracted a guard. 'What possessed you?'

'I took it,' Grace explained.

'Evidently, though I cannot fathom why.' Her big chestnut eyes twinkled. 'Are you, too, minded to meet an axe?'

'Anne – Her Majesty – bid me take it.' Grace considered the grand portrait, now propped up haphazardly against her bedpost. It depicted Anne wearing sumptuous emerald-green velvet robes, and her usual French hood lined with tiny pearls. It was an astonishing likeness: Master Hans had truly captured not only her beauty but also her warmth, her poise. It was Anne's favourite, and she had known that the king would have it destroyed.

While everything that had happened had happened quickly, in the weeks and days before Anne was unceremoniously escorted from court, there were little signs here and there; rumours and whispers. It's not only witches that can sense a coming change in the weather and, bit by bit, Anne's flame diminished as people wordlessly switched their allegiances. That ghastly locket Lady Seymour constantly fingered: *Everyone* knew who'd given it to her.

And so, as soon as she'd seen the carriages arrive to escort Anne to the Tower, Grace had created a small fire in the stables, a distraction, and while the men tended to it, she had liberated the portrait from the wall in the queen's gallery. She had secreted it in a concealed cabinet, disguised as a plain oak panel in Anne's drawing room. It could not remain in this hiding place. There wouldn't be many who knew of the vault's existence, but if Anne did, then the king did, and it was only a matter of time before her theft was discovered. She could only hope the guards presumed it had been destroyed with the rest when they came across the dark, empty oblong on the gallery wall.

Margery gazed down at the queen, and then at Grace herself, with solemn sympathy. Grace felt her hand, still icy from their flight, slip into her palm. 'I can see why Her Majesty would want something to survive her. Besides the princess, I mean. How else will people know her, remember her? The king . . . ' Margery chose her words carefully. 'The king seeks to erase her from legacy, as well as from court.'

'He will not succeed,' Grace said. 'I am assured of that.'

Margery too had been highly favoured by Anne. She was the daughter of the king's favourite musician, a trumpeter who'd first come to court from Spain with Queen Catherine when Margery was but an infant. De Leon, charming the king, was soon awarded an estate and land of his own. Admittedly quite tone-deaf, Margery took more after her mother, a skilled seamstress, and the emerald gown Anne wore for her sittings with Holbein had been, at least in part, embroidered by Margery.

'Can you get it out of court?' Grace asked, turning to her. 'You could enchant the guards, hide it until I can get it to the north.'

Margery frowned. 'And when will that be? I'm in no position to mind stolen wares. The shame it would cast upon my family . . . you ask a lot, Grace.'

Grace sighed. As an unmarried woman, Margery's position was more precarious. Grace herself was in no rush to return to her marital home, to her husband. Yorkshire held worse memories than even this sorry cage. Her duties at court were convenient in that sense; there was always a reason to stay. 'Soon,' she replied. 'I promise. When Cecilia is found and dealt with, I shall make my excuses and return to the manor.' Even with Anne gone, the thought of returning to Bingley filled her with dread.

Margery, it seemed, had only needed a moment to find her resolve. 'I apologise, sister. When have you ever asked me for anything? Very well. I shall take it to my father's estate tomorrow.'

Grace felt her shoulders sink in relief. Margery was a considerable witch; she had no doubt she could get the portrait away from court, and couldn't think of any reason why anyone would suspect her of theft. 'Thank you, sister, you have my favour.'

Margery reached out and tucked an errant lock of hair back under Grace's hood. 'If I may say: Sleep now, Grace.' Margery's eyes were wide, full of concern. 'I know how . . . fond you were of the queen, and how much she cherished . . . your loyalty. She would not want you in such tumult.'

Grace felt tears prick her eyes, but she swallowed back the painful lump in her throat. 'Margery . . . I am fine.'

'You can speak freely with me, Grace. About anything.'

Grace felt warm eyes search hers. The enchantress was trying to pry inside her, find emotions she'd stored far out of reach.

When Grace stayed silent, Margery stroked her cheek. 'If you will not talk, then at least *sleep*. I could help you, put you out.'

'No,' Grace said firmly. 'I will rest when Cecilia de la Torre is ash and dust.'

· ◯ ◑ ● ◑ ◯ ·

LADY GRACE FAIRFAX

Palace of Placentia - London

Grace cast a subtle glance at Margery's embroidery. It was masterful. Grace's own looked like a drunken spider had skittered over her tambour frame. The pair sat in the window seat overlooking the rose garden, a kind sun on their backs. It was a beautiful day, a farewell kiss from the summer.

Grace felt something unlock in her shoulders. This was *home* now.

Anne Boleyn entered the queen's chambers, freckled from the sunshine. Grace felt a modest delight, as she did every time Anne was close. 'Lady Margery, the king's tailor wishes to see you with some urgency.'

Margery rolled her eyes. The king was far more demanding than the queen when it came to his apparel. She set aside her embroidery. 'I shall attend to it.' Margery curtsied slightly for Anne. Grace wondered if she was even aware she'd done it. Anne was no more senior than Margery, and yet . . .

Things were changing.

'How is His Highness today?' Grace asked, fighting to maintain a breeziness in her tone. Anne smelled wonderful, her soap tinged with geranium, perhaps. It was most becoming.

Anne sidled into the space beside her in the window, fanning her skirts around her. 'It's a radiant day, is it not? The king is in fine spirits.' There was a satisfaction about Anne that made Grace furious. Outside the window, angry clouds started to clump in the sky. Anne could not be so blind as to ignore the fact he treated her rather better than anyone else at court. What Grace didn't know was if Anne was the *cause* of his recent ardour, as well as the *subject* of it. The speed with which the king had switched his affections from the other Boleyn sister to Anne was . . . questionable. Grace fought to keep her suspicions out of her mind, but it could so easily be witchcraft.

However, Grace had come to know Anne a little over the summer, and it just as easily might not be. *Everyone* wanted to be in Anne's company, herself included. That made sense, of course, with them both being witches.

Anne nudged her shoulder and said, 'Oh, cheer up, Grace! Soon it will be winter, and you can move clouds about to your heart's content. For now, at least, let us have our summer.'

'People are talking about you,' Grace chided.

'Let them.'

Increasingly, everyone else at court was in awe of Anne Boleyn. Grace wanted to be different to everyone else, at least in Anne's eyes, and so she thought to speak her truth. 'You ought mind yourself, Lady Anne. It's inappropriate.'

Anne pursed her lips. 'Is *that* all we have to aspire to in life? Propriety? I'm not sure that's what the likes of you or I were made for, are you?'

Grace couldn't argue with that. These last couple of months had been revelatory. Far from hiding their 'gifts', Anne, Jane, Nan, Margery and Cecilia flaunted their powers, albeit within the privacy of the coven. While at first it had been startling, Grace now found it intoxicating. A competitive streak she didn't even know she'd possessed emerged, and she found herself keen to not only impress the others but best them. The way they stood in awe as she lit the sky with lightning or drew forth tempest winds was addictive, and she noticed that the more she used her powers, the greater they became.

It was embarrassing, really, that she'd run from her birthright. Then again, she'd never had an Anne Boleyn in her life until now. Someone to show her the way. She'd learned so much in such a short amount of time: that there were *five* types of witch; that not all witches have the same fortitude; there were men with limited powers too; that there are witches all over the globe; even that there were places where women ruled. Grace was alone no longer.

'Where is the queen?' Anne now asked.

Grace discarded her own sewing. 'Where else? Confession.' All the queen did these days was confess. To what, Grace could not guess.

'I can,' Anne said, reading her thoughts. Grace cursed inwardly. She *had* to get better at shielding her mind. 'She bedded the king's brother, and that's why she hasn't been blessed with an heir.'

Grace fixed Anne with a doubtful glare. 'Come now. Really?'

Anne grinned. 'It's what the king believes, and that's as good as it being true, isn't it?'

Grace didn't dignify that with a response. She resumed her needlework instead.

'Your embroidery is improving,' said Anne.

'It isn't,' Grace told her. 'I always was hopeless.'

Anne reached for her hands, startling Grace. She flinched away from her, until she realised she was merely retrieving her sewing. Anne took the tambour off her and set about correcting her work. Grace felt herself flush. 'What were you like, as a wife?' said Anne.

She blushed even more deeply at that. 'What a question.'

'I'm not sure I've ever heard you speak of Lord Fairfax.'

'What is there to say?'

'Well,' Anne said, looking up from the embroidery. 'Did you marry for love?'

Grace didn't like this conversation or the sheer mass of Anne's stare. She felt herself shrink under it. 'I was thirteen, and a sheltered thirteen at that. I didn't know what love was.'

Anne smiled ever so slightly. 'And now you do?'

It wasn't worth saying anything. Anne already knew the answer.

· ○ ◑ ● ◐ ○ ·

LADY GRACE FAIRFAX

Hampton Court Palace - Middlesex

There was a brief moment, hazy seconds, where yesterday could have been some hideous dream. Grace's head had scarcely touched the pillow when dawn had arrived with its blackbirds and scullery maids. This was the closest in her life she had ever come to giving up, to just lying here and letting nature or the king take their course. What hope, what purpose, was left?

Only then did she feel the embers stoking. Anger.

She must find Cecilia.

She washed the sleep out of her face and, with the help of some chamber girls, dressed. The palace, and the sky outside the window, seemed watered down, thin. It was like some entire colour had gone out of the world.

She remained silent as they laced her corset. A grotesque pantomime. After what she'd seen last night in the slums, it felt only more obscene: dangling wealth off their skeletons, piling as much on their bodies as they could and hauling it around the palace like show ponies.

For as long as she could remember, Grace had wished she'd had the good fortune to be born a boy. Her parents had prayed for one, of that she'd been told countless times. If she'd been a boy, she'd have been called George. If she'd been a boy she'd have learned a trade – presumably in printing, her father's occupation. If she'd been a boy she wouldn't have been sold to Robert Fairfax, thirty-eight, when she was twelve. If, if, if. She had thought, back then, what was the good in being a witch, if one couldn't be who one wanted to be?

As it was, one girl secured her hair under a bonnet, plaiting it with dextrous fingers, while another fixed jewellery around her throat. At least she was the one being dressed; she ought to show some gratitude. 'Thank you,' she told them, almost too earnestly.

Alas, as expected, the most senior Lady of the Bedchamber, Lady Douglas, summoned all of the ladies-in-waiting ahead of breakfast in the queen's chambers. Meg Douglas was not a witch and, as far as Grace knew, had no inkling of their coven rituals. The Scot was only twenty-one, younger than many of the other ladies, but highly favoured by the king – he was her uncle, after all – and that was how she came to speak to them that morning.

Grace gathered amongst the other ladies, feeling crumpled, sticky-eyed, and hardly worthy of her post.

The news Meg brought came as no surprise to anyone. She delivered the information with a forced sunniness. 'His Majesty has asked Lady Seymour for her hand in marriage. There will be a formal announcement this morning. The wedding will take place at Whitehall in ten days' time.'

So there we are. Plain Jane would be queen.

No one said a word. How could they? It would border on treason in this airless climate. At her side, Margery instead took Grace's hand and gave it a gentle squeeze. Across the chambers, Grace briefly made eye contact with Jane Rochford. She too remained expressionless.

'I am quite sure,' Meg said, 'that we will all strive to serve the new queen however we can. Long may she reign.' Her words were loaded. This was what it was to serve a queen who in turn served a whimsical tyrant.

Grace wondered how the king would react if he were to learn Meg was courting Anne's uncle Tom Howard. It was an open secret. She pushed the petty thought aside, chastising herself for indulging in court gossip. After all these years, Grace ought to be immune. That said, surely Meg would put an end to the unauthorised union after the fate that had befallen Anne; who'd want to be associated with the witch queen? The girl looked as worn as Grace felt. She would have to bury it, the way Grace had buried so much of herself to survive court.

This was no place for love, or laughter, or soft bellies. They were all replaceable, even the queens. As they spoke, work was already underway in the Great Hall. Anne had not lived to see the renovations completed, but her herald – the falcon carvings in the wood – was already being knocked out by the king's craftsmen. In time they would be replaced with panthers for Seymour.

They went about their duties. The first task was to strip the queen's chambers of anything personal to Anne. Grace could not be seen to shed a tear, for so many reasons. She worked diligently in the bedchamber, ignoring Madge and Bess whispering as they tried to pocket some of Anne's trinkets. Let them, the fools. These keepsakes were not Anne. If anything, they were disguises.

'What do you think he loves in her?' Madge said cruelly. 'She's so dry.'

'I doubt it's love at all. Humourless,' Bess agreed. 'And so *ordinary*. Of all the pretty flowers in the garden . . . '

Grace eyed them with distaste. Two-faced scolds. Both women had switched sides to Jane Seymour over the slide of spring. 'We have work to do,' she snapped. Madge looked down her nose at her. She'd never liked Grace or her closeness to Anne. None of them had. Anne had many gifts, but her most potent had been her ability to make a person feel more special by proximity alone. Who wouldn't want that halo to bathe in? Alas, her having favourites had bred jealousy amongst her ladies.

Grace had her own theory about Lady Seymour; the king had blistered fingers. It made a depressing sort of sense that after the vivaciousness of Anne, he'd find solace in the austerity of Jane Seymour. She was something of a shrew about court, and certainly pious. Or maybe the king *was* listening, more than anyone realised. Truth was, as much as it pained Grace, Anne was not well liked. Maybe a meek queen would calm the nerves of the people. *The people* like a woman meek. Either way, that might spell concern for what was left of the coven.

Nonetheless, Grace could muster a modicum of sympathy for the incoming queen. The king had plucked another apple from the orchard; she hadn't much say in the outcome. Whether she had campaigned for it or not, the wheel of fate stopped now at Lady Seymour, and so it would come to pass.

Meanwhile, the crown had slipped through the coven's grasp. For now, at least. Grace wanted no business in Lady Rochford's machinations regarding the throne. Leave her to it.

Her idle thoughts were interrupted by a commotion coming from the Fountain Court. Men's voices, angry. A shrill cry, high and girlish, echoed through the palace. Grace shared a brief glance with Madge and Bess before they all wordlessly decided to investigate.

Emerging from the queen's apartments, she saw it was a brighter day than yesterday. The May sun illuminated the ornate archways surrounding the fountain. It didn't feel respectful that the Mother had forged ahead as swiftly as the king. On the sunny square, Grace watched as two stocky ruffians dragged young Temperance Wycliffe towards a strikingly tall man who waited on the lawn, a stranger, his peaked hat exaggerating his stature further. You wouldn't forget a face such as his. It was long, angular, something equine about it; his eyes black and distant.

Grace felt her stupid mouth hang open, fishlike and impotent. Grace did not know this slender man but understood at once his purpose in court. As she had feared; one witch was never enough.

Someone crashed into her shoulder, and Jane Rochford swept past her onto the square. Lucky one of them wasn't frozen. 'What is the meaning of this? Unhand her at once.'

The sweaty bookends either side of Temperance bade her kneel before the tall one. Staring down his beak nose, he didn't conceal his disdain for the girl. He turned his attention to Jane. 'And who might you be?'

'You shall address me as Viscountess Rochford,' Jane said, her eyes blazing and nostrils flared, 'and Lady Wycliffe is a member of the queen's bedchamber. You shall treat her as befits a lady of her status.'

'The *queen* is dead,' he said, and his meaning was apparent. If they could behead a queen, all bets were off. Status meant nothing any more.

Grace felt a buzz and a crackle about her hands. Could she make it look an act of God? Strike him down?

Jane briefly flustered. 'The, the *new* queen . . . we serve Lady Seymour. I say, what is your business here, sir?'

The stranger strode the perimeter of the babbling fountain as if it were a stage. 'My name is Sir Ambrose Fulke. I am the newly appointed witchfinder of the City of London. I come here at the behest of Lord Cromwell.' He lifted his proud nose to the air, as if sniffing them out. Grace prepared to kill him. She would if she had to; she found she could not care for self-preservation any more. The notion was briefly giddying. She ought to kill them all, cleanse this cursed palace with thunder and lightning. But what of her coven? No. No, she couldn't expose them so brutally. The wild abandon died down.

Her face almost to the grass, Temperance sobbed, her back shuddering. Had Cecilia betrayed her too? Temperance was a kind, sweet, if absent, girl. To turn her in for torture was unthinkable.

Fulke continued, pacing the courtyard in black boots so polished they flashed under the sun. All the king's men and all the queen's ladies now stood in the arches, audience to this strange theatre. 'There is sickness and rot here, my lords. The former queen, it transpires, was a worker of dark rites, her depraved fall expedited by the devil himself. Where there is one succubus, there are surely more, and the king is in great peril. This court must be purged of sin.'

Temperance looked up at her accuser. 'Please, my lord, I beg, I've done nothing wrong.'

He glowered. 'Lady Wycliffe, you stand accused of witchcraft diabolical.'

Jane helped Temperance to her feet. Grace stayed exactly where she was. Forming a group would only encourage the notion of a coven. 'An accusation she denies! Sir, this is folly.'

'It is said,' Fulke said, pausing to deliver his blow, 'Lady Wycliffe was observed in conversation with a fox at her night-time window.'

There was some immediate chatter among the onlookers. It took Grace every ounce of strength not to bark an incredulous whoop. Not even the most powerful enchantress could speak with the animals, and in any case, Temperance was a sorceress. But women had been killed on far thinner evidence than that.

'It's not true!' Temperance protested.

This could go on no longer. Jane intervened. Her voice changed; it was calm, measured, hypnotic. 'Sir Ambrose, hear me, you are gravely mistaken. A clear case of false witness.' She looked deep inside him, writing her truth over his. 'Temperance is not the girl you seek.'

Grace did what she could. It was easy enough to bring about a sudden chill to such a small yard. Some ladies hurried back inside, rubbing their arms. Icicles formed in the fountain. From the margins, Margery and Isabel helped as well. The enchantresses surreptitiously joined hands, combining their will. *Return to your duties*, Margery seeded the notion throughout the courtyard. *This matter is resolved.*

Almost sleepily, the courtiers and servants sighed little clouds of frost breath, and went back to work.

Jane continued to weave in Fulke. 'Temperance is a God-fearing girl. She takes the sacrament every day, my lord.'

The man seemed strong, bitterly resolved to his mission.

Concerning. Grace looked to Margery, who half shrugged. And then Fulke took off his hat, holding it afront his heart apologetically. 'My lady,' he said to Temperance. 'I can only apologise for my men's roughness. It seems we have been woefully misinformed.'

Temperance wiped away her tears. 'Dear sir, you slander me.'

He bowed his head further. 'I ask your forgiveness in this matter.'

'I grant it,' she said, under duress as Jane squeezed her arm.

'May I suggest, Sir Ambrose,' said Jane, 'that you might focus your endeavours on the wilds to the north, and Scotland, where feral women roam the moors and heaths. There are *no witches at court*,' she added powerfully.

Grace thought of her aunt in Yorkshire. Far from wild, far from feral.

Fulke put his hat back atop his head and, for a moment, seemed suspicious once more. 'I am afraid I do not share your confidence, viscountess. There is wickedness afoot, mark my words.' Oh, that, Grace could accept. And then he grew more confident still. He spoke directly to Jane. 'I shudder to think of the rancour you saw sharing a home as you did with your debauched husband. It is a small wonder you remain as virtuous as you say.'

Jane bristled, her lips trap-tight. Anything she said would only mire her. Grace couldn't take it any longer. She stepped forth. 'Lady Rochford. We have urgent business with Lady Seymour.'

Fulke sighed, seemingly accepting this. 'You would do well, my lady, to remain vigilant.'

Gratitude ebbed from Jane. She curtsied to the witchfinder. 'That I shall, Sir Ambrose. I shall keep you in my prayers.'

'Thank you. Apologies once more, Lady Wycliffe.'

Jane's voice was already in Grace's head: *Chapel – at once.*

Leave.

The chaplain duly wandered out of his own chapel at Jane's command. At this time of day, with court thrumming, no one would miss them – they would make sure of it. What remained of their coven gathered: Grace, Jane, Margery and Temperance, young Isabel and Old Nan Cobb. The candles, the myrrh, always made Grace's eyes feel gluey.

'What are we to do?' Temperance said, still quivering. Nan held her close, almost cradling the girl at her bosom, as they perched on the step before the altar.

'The impudence!' Jane seethed. 'Marching into the palace and hurling accusations of witchcraft.'

'We *are* witches,' Margery said, and Grace laughed, despite everything.

'We are still noblewomen of this court!' snapped Jane, in no mood for humour. For the first time, Grace saw some of the last few days spill out. Understandable that she, of all of them, would need to believe there was still a place for her here. Anne had ingratiated her father, her brother, and his wife into the highest echelons of court. Now Jane Rochford found herself on perilously thin ice.

Grace said, 'With respect, Jane, if these atrocious weeks have a lesson it is thus: we are all of us vulnerable. Even the queen.' There was a cold silence, and no one went to contradict her. 'Sir Ambrose Fulke is the shape of things to come. Not the king, nor Cromwell, created this fever, they merely seized upon it. As it is now, if you name a woman a witch with enough conviction, she is a woman no more, let alone a lady. We should all be afeared.'

Margery sat on a pew, head in her hands. 'What do you propose?'

Grace steeled herself. 'Anne's great vision lies in tatters. Our purpose is elsewhere now. I say we deal with the traitor as is the way of witches. Then we bid farewell to this insufferable viper's nest once and for all.'

'Lunacy!' Jane started, but Grace went on.

'No! What reason have we here now? Bending and scraping to the whims of a tyrant?' She looked to Jane. 'You are *powerful*, sister, they need never know we were here, need never know we left, need never know we lived. We can map our own course from here.'

'I am Viscountess Rochford,' Jane stated proudly.

'For now,' Grace said, and instantly wished she'd held her tongue. She felt an invisible force slam into her middle and she fell backwards, sliding across the cold, hard floor.

'Stop this!' Nan chided. 'Last thing we need.'

Grace scowled at Jane, who apologised as she helped her to her feet. 'I am sorry, sister,' Jane muttered, shamefaced.

Nan was right. It would reward only the men for them to turn on each other. 'I spoke out of turn,' Grace said.

'I was a noblewoman before I met my husband and I remain so. Like it or not, this is my home, Lady Fairfax. It's all I have ever known.'

'I cannot leave my mother and father,' Margery added softly. 'Nor should I have to.'

Grace could argue with neither. She found herself envying those feral, moor-wandering hags. She realised the rest of the coven *liked* their lives. She saw it in all their eyes. That must be nice for them. They pitied her, these women, her sisters – and they were all she had left in the world. She realised *that* was why she was so consumed with hatred for Cecilia; she had trusted her.

There was a chill at her core, and Grace couldn't so much as imagine a summer. How could she, now she was without Anne. There wasn't a reason for Grace Fairfax any more.

✦ ○ ◑ ● ◐ ○ ✦

LADY GRACE FAIRFAX

Bisham Manor - Berkshire

By the time they reached the countess's country home, evening was almost upon them. By daylight, it was too much to risk flight, and so the women rode one of the queen's carriages out of London and into the lush green pastures of Berkshire.

The manor was an amiable-looking, red-roofed structure, not dissimilar to Grace's own marital home in Yorkshire. Accepting the help of a groomsman, Grace disembarked the coach behind Jane.

Lady Margaret Pole was, of course, expecting them, either by magic or by logic. She greeted their carriage in the courtyard, a vision of hospitality in a russet gown and rubies at her collar. 'Viscountess, Lady Fairfax, you have travelled far. To what do I owe the pleasure?'

Grace was in no mood for pleasantries. It had been a long, uneven journey spent in close quarters with a woman she was scarcely fond of. 'Do you wish me to say in front of your household staff?'

'Come.' Pole smiled tersely. 'I shall ask the kitchen to prepare us some supper.'

Safely in the privacy of the dining room, and with a fire crackling in the hearth, Grace accepted some goose and bread and a small cup of mead. She hadn't eaten since they'd left the queen's quarters at the Tower, and now she felt hollow and ethereal. She couldn't afford to fall ill. The food felt hard-edged inside her, almost painful after her fast.

'You know why we're here,' Jane said, dabbing her mouth on a handkerchief.

'She isn't here,' Margaret said without hesitation.

'She was.' Jane was the stronger witch; she'd be able to read the countess. It was fruitless for Margaret to attempt a lie. 'Where is she now?'

Margaret raised a goblet to her lips with thin fingers. 'She left with the dawn. To where I know not.'

'Please don't lie to me, Margaret, you do us both a disservice.'

'You know her crime,' Grace said, wishing she hadn't had the mead. Her tongue felt reckless. 'And yet you harboured her.'

'I did no such thing. I wrote to Jane by candlelight and sent a messenger to court. It seems likely you crossed him on your journey here. When you receive this letter, you shall see how I swiftly informed you of Lady de la Torre's whereabouts. I intended to detain her until such a time that you came for her.'

Grace and Jane shared a doubtful glance.

'It's true!' Pole protested. 'Every word. Cecilia is a powerful young witch. She must have sensed my true intentions and fled.'

'Why would you act such?' Jane said.

'You loathed the queen's union to the king,' added Grace. 'You loathed the queen.'

'I am loyal to my coven.'

Another dubious claim. 'What is it you want, Lady Pole?' Jane Rochford said, clearly bored of the exchange. Grace too felt the fug of tiredness seep in. She'd expected to apprehend, if not execute, Cecilia de la Torre this night. Now that was looking unlikely.

'I want,' Margaret said, her voice now quavering, 'a return to court.'

Grace couldn't hide her surprise. 'My lady, would that be wise?' Catholicism was perhaps the only matter held in lower regard at court than witchcraft.

'I must. I cannot have this shame hang over my family name a moment longer.'

Jane looked haughtily down her nose at the Countess of Salisbury. 'You would betray your faith so quickly. And what of Mary?'

'I serve only the king.' Only three years prior, Margaret had offered to serve the king's eldest daughter without recompense. The Catholic daughter of the old Catholic queen, a relic now, a curio. Her pleas had gone unheeded. The king thought precious little of the Pole family. 'Though I confess the princess is often in my prayers.'

'The word *princess* is pretty, but it's treason,' Grace said. 'You flirt with the axe, my lady. You'd be safer here in exile.'

Margaret took her goblet to the fireplace. 'They are children, Lady Fairfax. Mary, Elizabeth, the Fitzroy boy: They are innocents in all this. It mustn't be forgotten. They didn't ask to be placed at court; fate dealt them these ill cards.'

It was with wretched guilt that Grace only now considered the whereabouts of the young Princess Elizabeth. Would she still be at Hatfield? Her mother's death, and the king's forthcoming marriage, would beyond any doubt erase her already flimsy position at court. Mary had been declared a bastard. The same would surely befall Anne's daughter. To think of the child, and how much Anne had adored her, hurt more than Grace liked. Not for the first time, it was the sour milk of jealousy.

To envy an infant. Pathetic.

Margaret was still protesting her fealty. 'I accept the king and I embrace his faith. It is right I should serve the new queen.'

Jane finished her mead in a masculine gulp. 'Very well. Then where is the traitor?'

Countess Pole turned to them. 'She seeks passage to the continent. She will make haste to the sea.'

NOW – 20 MAY 1536

LADY CECILIA DE LA TORRE

The Port of Dover - Kent

Mindful of the watchful eyes of the grey castle atop the cliffs, Cecilia disguised herself as a nobleman, weaving amongst the merchants and sailors of the dock. The enchantment was powerful but exhausting. She wouldn't be able to maintain it for long.

Three single-mast ships and a larger two-sail were docked in port and the air was salty, pungent from damp nets and lobster pots. It wasn't unpleasant or unfamiliar, reviving memories of that first voyage to England in her girlhood.

'Good sir.' She stopped a more senior-looking shipman from the larger vessel. 'Could you direct me to your captain?'

'I suggest you try the inn, my lord.'

Cecilia did not need the approval of a captain, she could easily stow away undetected. What she required was information. 'Which of the vessels sets out first?' she instead asked.

The false countenance she wore fluctuated, but he perceived her as male, handsome. In fact, this sailor was more than a little attracted to her in this form. A vivid pink light sizzled within him; desire.

At the same time, he looked perplexed, surprised perhaps at her ignorance. 'My lord, we will not sail tonight. The tides are against us.'

Cecilia fought to hide her frustration. So be it.

'Perhaps I shall see you later for a bevy?'

'Perhaps indeed.' Cecilia had no desire to see the sailor again in any context. Instead, she pulled her hood up and headed for the inn on the marketplace.

It didn't take long to identify the captain, already several tankards deep by the hearth, and establish that tomorrow he would sail from Dover to Southampton. From there, he said, she could secure passage across the Bay of Biscay and through the Mediterranean to Venice. It would be a long voyage, but with a kind wind, she'd be out of the reach of the coven in a day.

Still incognito, Cecilia ordered a goblet of wine – the inn had an impressive selection straight off the boats from Bordeaux – and settled herself at the bar. No one would pay her any heed. She took a sip of the wine. It was plump and fruity. It reminded her of their summer in Kent; the year the sweating sickness had swept the country, forcing the coven into exile at Anne's family home.

Anne had liked her wine, and so did Cecilia. Once Anne was

recovered, they'd sampled many of the bottles from the cellar, bonding over their shared tastes. Grace didn't enjoy grape or grain the way they did. Cecilia remembered trying to interest her, trying to teach her the subtle differences between the French and Spanish wines. It had been in vain.

It all tastes alike to me.

You're a philistine, Grace Fairfax.

I had no such luxuries growing up. I never want to get too used to them, lest this all goes away through some dreadful misfortune.

What an austere way to exist! We are here now, and these moments are to be savoured. Indulge yourself, Grace . . .

There was a man staring intently at her across the tavern. His wiry red hair was long, braided. She directed his attention elsewhere, but he belligerently held her gaze. He unmounted his stool and made for her position. A warlock. Curses. Of all the rotten luck. 'I mean no trouble,' she told him, her voice low. He could see her for who she was. For a man, he held considerable power.

'I came with a silver coin to pay for your wine,' he said. 'I mean to toast your health, Lady de le Torre.'

How did he know who she was? She fought to remain poised. 'Thank you, kind sir, but I prefer to drink alone.'

'But I insist.'

She sighed. Why do they always try twice? Why is the first time never sufficient? 'Do I know you, sir?'

'Samuel Popper, at your service.' The man had watercolour

eyes, blue-grey. There was a shrewd smirk on his mouth. 'We have not met, but I have friends at court, and I heard your thoughts quite well. You give yourself away.'

Cecilia stiffened. 'I know not of what you speak.'

'Liar. Oh, I mean you no harm, pretty one. You did the warlock clans a great favour by ridding us of the queen. She moved against our Catholic brethren.'

'I did no such thing.'

'Why lie, my lady?'

There had been a time, it is said, before civilisation, when witches and warlocks had not just coexisted but worked as one in harmony. But with the indomitable spread of angry-man-of-the-sky religion, there came new ideas about how men should be and how women should be. Suddenly, the men did not like that the women were the more gifted, more magical, more powerful. Division arose. The church backed them as men, so women sought refuge, solidarity and sisterhood in their covens and the men . . . well, the magi descended into messy little factions and massacred their neighbours. Sad, really.

Cecilia took a decent slug of her wine. 'Mr Popper, my actions had nothing to do with your trifling concerns. Nor did the queen's, for that matter. She fought only for the progress of witchkind. All ships rise with the tide and her aims were your aims, surely?'

'I doubt the word *mage* crossed her lips more than twice in her whole life.' The warlock took a sip of his ale. 'You sound admiring of her.'

Cecilia shrugged.

'Your actions betray you. Why did you serve her head thus?'

She didn't owe this man an explanation. She finished her wine and went to leave. She would sleep aboard the ship.

'You did it for love.' Popper grasped her arm. He'd read her. He sneered under his breath. '*Women.*'

'Unhand me.' When he did not, she took hold of his wrist with her mind and bent it sharply back. He was strong, but she was stronger by far. With a satisfying clack, he wrenched his hand away.

'Bitch!' he snarled. 'What if I alert the queen's coven?'

'You won't even remember I was here, Samuel Popper.' She placed a hand to his head and erased the entire exchange from his beer-addled mind.

Cecilia swept away from the bar and went to leave the tavern. She would bed down for the night, find some secret, comforting spot on the vessel bound for Southampton and lie low.

She was only two strides outside the tavern when the men slid out of the shadows like alley cats. Instinctively she went to halt them, casting her command about herself like a shield. The men stumbled but continued to struggle towards her, forcing themselves against her psychic barrier.

'I said *halt*.' She clamped her teeth together, pushed harder.

The men were magi. Individually, she could better them, but

there were three of them and but one of her. Popper must have alerted his clan. A vulgar lot they were too, unwashed and red-knuckled.

'Witch,' one said. 'What have you done to our friendly Popper?'

'He is unharmed.' It took everything to hold them at arm's length. 'Let me go and it shall remain so.'

A man with a silver beard almost to his belly stepped into the lantern light. 'Big words for such a small lady. Look at you, never done a day's work in your life.'

She released her grip on all of them in order to throw him back towards the quay, and he collided with the sea defences, crying out in pain. Cecilia prepared to launch herself into the night sky, but arms clamped around her chest. 'Unhand me!'

'I think not, my lady.' Behind her, Samuel Popper squeezed her tight. 'Your spell almost worked. *Almost.*'

Cecilia couldn't breathe. 'Please. Please I beg.'

I like my women to beg. His words filled her head as the night went black.

SIR AMBROSE FULKE

Esher Palace - Surrey

Fulke, shirtless, was on his knees before Christ on the cross. His private chapel, off the bedroom. The king had offered Fulke and his men the use of Cardinal Wolsey's former estate, just a few miles from Hampton Court. Many of his holy effects remained, including this sanctum. A rosary tightly bound his pale fingers; palms clasped in prayer.

'O Holy Lord, enlighten me thus. Illuminate your righteous path and show me the way to work your will on earth as it is in Heaven.'

He screwed his eyes shut, longing for the fullness he had felt, once. The time the Holy Spirit had filled him. His epiphany, two winters hence. While fasting and ridden with fever, the truth had enveloped him in the midst of the night. The Lord God spoke to him in the form of an archangel, a celestial being with the body of a man and the head of a great white bull with horns of gold. As the words entered his mind, Fulke saw things plain. The greatest degradation of man, and the path to salvation.

It was women.

Women were ungodly. They had fallen from virtue in Eden, irrevocably tainted.

Repented women had value as wives and mothers, but not all repent.

Women were by definition sullied, and witches were the worst of them, consorts of the devil.

The devil women must be purged from the garden.

He looked up at Christ's hollow face. 'Where are they, my Lord? Where are these infernal whores of Satanis? My purpose is clear, oh Lord, but why do you abandon me now? I feel you no longer inside my breast. I feel nothing . . . nothing! You leave me cold. I pray in the name of the Father, the Son and the Holy Ghost, fill me once more. Guide my hand.'

The crucifix fell from between his palms, and Fulke let it dangle over the candle on the shrine.

'The queen of blasphemies, the despicable Anne Boleyn, is dead. She languishes in the fires of hell. Come to me now, my Lord, reveal unto me the names of her diabolical accomplices. I will purge them, my Lord; I will rid your garden of their rot.'

Fulke bent over, his forehead pressed painfully to the cold tiles.

'Lilith and Eve and all thereafter; their sinful stain a distraction from your holy light. I see it for what it is, oh Lord. It is the great battle. Heaven awaits in abstinence and asceticism.'

He looked up once more into the gaunt, pained face of Christ, his silent scream eternal. 'I am yours, Heavenly Father.'

The silver crucifix glowed red in the flame. Fulke impressed it to his chest and let his flesh burn in the name of Christ.

• ○ ◗ ● ○ ○ •

LADY GRACE FAIRFAX

Hever Castle - Kent

What is it, do you suppose, Anne had asked, *the men think we do when they are out of sight?*

Whatever the men's assumption, the truth was they played cards or merels, and drank wine, and sang songs before the fire. Down here, away from court, and with a household staff handpicked by Anne herself, they could also practise their craft quite freely. The women wore chemises and bedroom gowns instead of their corsets and farthingales, because who was here to see them.

Grace felt as free, and as content, as she had ever in her whole life. How she had carried that sadness with her. She wasn't aware of its burden until she was rid of it.

The coven had been sequestered away from London early into the summer, seeking refuge from the English Sweat. Panic had set about court: a king without a legitimate male heir cannot afford to die. Anne herself had fallen sick, but after the king sent his personal physicians, she was swiftly healed. Nan Hobbs, of course, had already attended to her, but the king wasn't to know that.

This summer of frivolity couldn't last forever. Sooner or later, they would have to return to court, and every time Grace thought about it, she felt waterlogged within. In Kent, the king felt very far away, little more than a story they all knew.

Hever was Anne's family home, and here there was no other queen to contend with. 'Let us form a circle.' She pushed aside her armchair to create space on the rug. She was merry, unsteady on her feet after much wine. 'Come, join hands.'

Anne held out her hand to Grace. She accepted it and seated herself at Anne's right. A right-hand woman. It was no secret that Queen Catherine's days were numbered, and at a time when everyone was picking sides, Grace was aware of how she was regarded: a Boleyn devotee. But it was not courtly manoeuvring; Grace held no animosity towards Catherine whatsoever, she just preferred Anne's company. It was no more complicated than that.

And, of course, they had something in common.

A couple of things, in truth. On reflection, it *was* complicated. At least for Grace; Anne was as unbothered as she ever was.

The other women joined them in the circle. Lady Boleyn – Jane – locked the door before doing the same. A powerful coven they were now. A young witch of just fifteen years, Lady

Temperance Wycliffe, had come to court mere weeks before the sickness broke out. Another sorceress, and one with great promise. It was nice, Grace thought, not to be the fledgling member of their circle any longer.

Temperance now joined Cecilia on the hearth alongside Margery and Nan. Seven, as any witch will tell you, is a powerful number. Indivisible, as was their coven.

'Let us join,' Anne said.

Each witch closed their eyes, and Anne started to hum. She was a beautiful singer. Her wandering aria lulled them into one mind. Anne once told her she made them up based on how she felt that night. Tonight's ballad was airy, sleepy and gentle, almost a feather against Grace's cheek. She was very familiar with Anne's radiance by now: peacock blue with amber lightning. Grace let it migrate through her soul.

I feel her, Anne told them all, *I feel the Mother, the creator of all things. She hears our song. She is us, and we are her. She will not steer us wrong in our endeavours.*

Anne squeezed Grace's hand more tightly. The circle left the floor, spirit flowing through them, and lifting them up. Grace felt her bare feet dangling in free air but was held firm. So much conversation at court concerned power, but this was *real* power.

Her aunt had taught Grace of the Mother as a child, but now she could *feel* her. She felt *held,* safe with her coven. This was who she was meant to be.

'Grace,' Anne said. 'Wait a while.'

It was time for bed, almost dawn in fact, but Anne held her back as the others drifted to their bedchambers.

'I want to show you something.' Anne's eyes were glassy and her face slack. She'd had too much wine. So had Grace, probably. The room billowed a little as she stood.

All the same, Grace felt a familiar high of being Anne's confidante. The chosen. To be chosen by anyone is a tickle; to be chosen by her was a treasure.

Anne took her hand and led her through the darkened corridors to her bedchamber. As they ran down the halls, they laughed at the top of their lungs, too merry to care if anyone slept. With Grace shushing Anne, they came to her bedchamber. It was one of the larger chambers, with a private garderobe and chapel adjoining. 'What is it you wanted to show me?' Grace asked, breathless from their flit.

'Light some candles, will you?' Anne asked. When Grace stalled, she turned back to her in the gloom. 'You can do it. You can do anything. I trust you.'

Grace swallowed and held out a palm to create a spark hot enough to light a candle, but not so hot that it would burn down the entire castle. Fire is chaos by nature and, by nature, Grace was not.

She focused on one candle and it popped to life. It wasn't even hard. This *fear* was real though; nothing imagined could take up so much space. Instead of using her gifts, she used the first candle to light the others. 'What did you wish to show me?'

'Look!' Anne crouched at her bedside, as if in prayer, and withdrew a bundle of letters from underneath her mattress. She handed the correspondence to Grace. 'They're from the king . . . '

Even down here, he'd caught up to her. With trepidation, Grace withdrew a sheet of parchment. The paper felt almost velveteen on her fingers. Grace recognised his curiously feminine script from countless declarations. The language she recognised as French, which she scarcely spoke a word of. 'What are they?'

'Proclamations. Of his feelings. For me.' Candlelight danced in Anne's eyes. That explained the French. He was showing off.

Grace was more than experienced when it came to keeping feelings off her face. She'd mastered it over a lifetime of disappointments. After two years at court, she'd become very skilled at keeping enchantresses out of her mind, too. 'How wonderful.'

None of this came as a surprise to Grace. She had eyes and used them. Anyone could see the way the weather had changed in court. Poor *Catarina*, the queen now in name alone, increasingly drifting into a frozen wasteland, while Anne bathed in the summer sun of the king's affections. He scarcely bothered to conceal his intentions towards Anne, and why would he? Who was there to challenge him? Least of all God.

'Would you like to hear what he says?'

'No!' Grace said far too quickly. 'Rather, I feel . . . it would betray his privacy.'

Anne lowered her voice to a whisper. 'He intends to marry me, Grace.'

Grace folded the letter and thrust it back into Anne's hands. She wanted none of this stink on her. 'Anne, my sister, these letters are treason.'

'How? When they are from the throne?'

'The queen . . . '

A rehearsed sigh, an imitation of sympathy, passed her lips. 'I love the queen, as do we all, but we must also acknowledge the truth, plain as it is. She was married to the king's brother, and she is a widow. She wasn't fit to be queen in the first instance, a dreadful mistake.'

The words escaped Grace's mouth before she could stop them. 'And you are fit?'

Luckily, Anne grinned back. 'Oh, sweet Grace!' She pushed herself up onto the bed. 'Don't look so scandalised! Sit with me.'

Grace looked to the door, wishing she'd had the sense to take to her bed with the others.

'Come, sit.' Anne patted the empty expanse of bedding alongside her. It felt an inappropriate space for such a conference, the sheets smooth and pristine. Grace relented and joined Anne, perching on the very rim of the bed. 'Tell me, sister. What do you know of pleasure?'

Grace felt her face redden. Anne knew she was married. 'I know of men.'

A smile. 'Then you know nothing of pleasure.' Grace was about to argue, but Anne continued. 'When I was in France, in the court of Queen Claude, I learned many things. Court there is an altogether more eclectic beast, you see, and perhaps the most important lesson was that of men, and of women in the world of men.'

Grace sat stiffly on the bed, her feet not quite touching the floor. 'I'm not certain what you mean,' she said.

'Oh, stop it!' Anne took her hands and hauled her into the heart of the mattress. They lay next to each other, side to side and face-to-face. The bedlinen was cool on her bare legs. 'I think you do.'

Grace said nothing. It was most peculiar being so close to another woman, their noses only inches apart. It was more intense than she could stand. Almost.

Anne didn't seem to care. 'You saw the fate of my sister, Mary, did you not? At the hands of the king, and in the eyes of the court. A mistake I am not keen to repeat.' She squeezed her hands, as if to impress the importance of her words. 'Women are a fiction, Grace. We are a story we tell to men. The trick, as with any good story, is to captivate the reader. Shall I tell you how I have captivated the king?'

Grace already knew.

A dance at court, only three months hence, before the sweating sickness had taken hold of London. How could anyone *not* be entranced by Anne as she danced? She was a swan on a pond of coots. It was there, at that dance, as the king remained glued to Anne's hand, blithely ignoring dignitaries and princes, that Grace had realised this was no idle infatuation. With every twirl and revolution around the ballroom, Anne's eyes had found Grace's amidst the merrymaking. How did she do that? Make *everyone* feel seen, all at once. A gift greater than her witchcraft.

'Tell me,' Grace said, her voice snagging in her throat.

Anne looked up at her under hooded eyes, coy, and beguiling. 'Like this. I remain a mystery. I am whatever his imagination needs me to be. I'm the only thing in this world he can't have, and it's killing him. So yes, in answer to your question, I am *fit* to marry.'

'But why, Anne? Why play this tiresome game?'

Anne scowled. 'Is it not a game you played with Lord Fairfax?'

Grace shifted, uneasy. Without a doubt she had benefitted from being the *second* Lady Fairfax. Her husband's precious male heirs had been older than she herself when they'd married. It'd been enough that she was young, pristine and fair on the day of their nuptials. By the time her husband was disappointed in her frigidity, it was already too late – the ring was on her finger. So no, no she had never been anything but herself. Grace told her so.

'Don't you see?' Anne said as though it were evident. 'I do all this for *us*. For the coven. No more hiding what we are.'

Grace could bite her tongue no longer. 'My sister, with respect; our kind have never been welcomed. Feared then, and feared still.'

'Because we toil in shadow like ghouls and demons. Well, no more. The world, in good time, will see the truth of things. We are glorious.'

Anne, as if pleased with herself, leapt off the bed. She crossed to her dresser and let down her hair. Taking a brush in hand she tended to her long locks. Grace stood and went to help, taking the ivory brush from her. 'And what of you?'

'What of me?'

'The king has made his feelings plain. Where is your heart?'

For a moment, Anne said nothing, the crunch of the comb scraping through hair the only sound in the bedchamber. 'I find him appealing enough.'

He's an overgrown toddler, Grace told her, not using her tongue.

Anne laughed, covering her mouth. 'Now who speaks treason?' She smiled.

'I said naught,' Grace smiled back into the mirror.

'Queen Claude, very wise, once told me monarchs are eternally frozen on the day they are crowned. I suppose that means the king is forever seventeen.'

That seemed accurate from Grace's observations.

'The king is handsome. Tall. He has many admirable qualities.'

'He's dangerous.' Grace stated the obvious.

'He has a manner with ladies,' Anne said, and Grace snorted. 'It's true! He spent his entire childhood with his mother and sisters. I have met far worse, believe me.'

Suddenly, Anne winced and Grace realised the brush was tangled in her hair. 'I'm sorry,' Grace said, setting the tool aside.

The conversation sat heavy in Grace's stomach and she felt sickly on it. Outside, thunder growled, and furious winds pummelled the turrets of Hever Castle. Ghosts seemed to wail about the walls.

'Sister, do not fret.' Of course, there was only so much Grace could conceal from Anne. She was at a constant disadvantage.

Grace rested a hand on Anne's shoulder and Anne stroked it reciprocally. 'Alas, I do.'

She went to turn away before Anne could explore the depths of her anxiety, but Anne caught her hand before she could remove it. 'Then find solace in this.' Anne's lips brushed lightly against Grace's fingers. 'I am here.'

LADY GRACE FAIRFAX

Bisham Manor - Berkshire

On this, the second day after Anne's death, Grace awoke in a sore skin. Everything hurt; the pillowcase, the blankets. Everything felt too solid, too harsh, too real. This was the world now. What a pointless place it was.

The sun climbed up the windows and Grace washed and summoned a dresser. As was correct, she would join Countess Pole for breakfast before departing.

As Grace waited for her hostess in the dining hall, she became aware of the first footman lingering over her shoulder, a yard into the room. 'Sir?'

'I'm sorry, my lady,' he said, chin almost touching his chest. 'I thought, if the moment was opportune, how I should like to pay my respects.'

Grace inhaled, somehow surprised. There had been no kind

words for the queen at court. 'Thank you, sir.' They were the only two in the hall. 'There are not many who'd share such sentiments in public. Least of all in this household.'

The footman, a handsome man with a strong jaw and nose, checked over his shoulder once more. 'I was fond of the queen and *acquainted* with her brother. I previously served at Hever.' Ah, that was where she recognised him from.

'Yes, I was fond of her too,' Grace admitted, and she wondered if this servant knew this ache she felt today. George's execution felt like a century ago. How many days had passed in reality? Only five.

Grace had no more questioned Lord Rochford's whereabouts than he had questioned hers and Anne's, although there were persistent wasp-like rumours around George Boleyn. Weren't there always? He had a roguish air, but she had liked him. He was quick-humoured, and naughty. Anne adored her big brother. It had been all too easy for Cromwell to spin his disgusting lies, and for fools to believe them.

'Thank you for your kind words,' she said. They were interrupted by the arrival of a serving girl. The candid moment was concluded. As the footman tended to his business, Grace stopped him. 'Wait. Where is Lady Rochford? Will she be joining us for breakfast?'

The footman seemed confused. 'I apologise, my lady, I thought you knew. The viscountess left before the dawn. She told me not to rouse you.'

Grace felt her heart quicken, some unnamed dread taking hold of her throat. 'Did she give a reason for her departure?'

The footman told her she had not. Grace was no seer, but it felt like things had just got that much worse. Dark clouds gathered over Bisham like a shroud.

SIR AMBROSE FULKE

Esher Palace - Surrey

It was Aristotle who said, *Man is by nature a social animal; an individual who is unsocial naturally and not accidentally is either beneath our notice or more than human. Society is something that precedes the individual. Anyone who either cannot lead the common life or is so self-sufficient as not to need to, and therefore does not partake of society, is either a beast or a god.*

As such, Fulke was not surprised to find the Lady Rochford darkening his door. She thought she was above them all. She wore her sins brazenly as jewellery; pride, avarice, vainglory. They would be her downfall. He would never utter it aloud, but the king too would benefit from walking amongst the people again. A reminder he was beast, not god.

Fulke circled her as she sat stiff in a chair, fingering a lace handkerchief. 'This isn't easy for me, my lord,' she said. He would have guessed she would be first to snivel out of the woodwork. She had the most to lose, and was the nearest to the precipice.

Her husband's loathsome desires were well known. It was unthinkable she was ignorant to his strange appetites, and thus she wilfully looked away from his sins. *As for those who persist in sin, rebuke them in the presence of all so that the rest may stand in fear.*

'What is it you wish to confess Lady Rochford?'

The woman looked at him now, unrepentant, a glint of anger in her green eyes. 'I confess before the Lord, Sir Ambrose. I come before you not in supplication but in the spirit of charity.'

He could not bear it, this mimicry of fey softness. Quite pathetic. He understood *why* the womenfolk entered into it, for it was their lot, but it was trickery. A woman is a mace, wrapped in velvet. Woe betide any man who fell for it. 'Ah, I see,' he purred. 'And what is it you bring me so generously?'

She sat upright. 'Contrary to the tattle of idle tongues, I was shocked and disgusted when I learned of the . . . actions of my husband and the queen. If I am guilty of anything, it's innocence, my lord. How could I have known what I was marrying into? Their dark artistry, their . . . European manner.'

'Is that so?' Desperation. Florid, steaming desperation. To spout such feculence, she must truly fear for her life at court. Such was the way under this king. Even his closest friends and allies fell in and out of favour with almost seasonal regularity. Interesting that the Boleyn woman saw him as her path to redemption. Only God would save her. It was his duty to set her on the righteous path.

He crouched at her side, wary still. 'Lady Rochford. Were you aware the queen practised witchery?'

'No!' she almost sobbed. 'I was never close to her. I came to court in service of Queen Catherine, the good and worthy.'

He sensed there was more. 'Say what it is you want to say, my lady.'

'There was a darkness in Anne Boleyn. She walked by night, my lord,' she breathed. 'And she was not alone.'

He knew it. Witches find strength in cohorts. 'Who? Tell me now.'

Rochford shook her head. 'Understand, I pray. If I disclose her allies, I paint a target about myself. There's no telling what these harridans will do to me, my lord.'

He crossed to his writing desk and slapped a parchment and quill before the woman on the side table. 'Names, my lady. Produce a list of names and never again will you live in fear. They shall be snuffed.'

Jane Boleyn, Lady Rochford, the viscountess, or whatever name she wore now, took the pen and dipped it in the inkwell. The nib scratched across the paper. He didn't, for a second, believe Rochford was a simpering widow with a head full of daisies. But that didn't mean court limpets weren't of value to him. Quite the contrary.

She slid her page across the desk to him.

There was but one name on the parchment. It read: *Lady Cecilia de la Torre.*

NOW – 21 MAY 1536

LADY CECILIA DE LA TORRE

The Mermaid Inn, Rye - East Sussex

She awoke to the earthen, herbaceous tang of hops. Ale and black mould. A cellar. A beer cellar. She was gagged, and there was something on her tongue, something sharp and bitter-tasting. There was a bridle secured around her face, leather straps cutting into the flesh of her cheeks. She allowed herself a confused second before she whipped out with everything she had.

The whole building, wherever she was, shook. Samuel Popper withdrew a bollock dagger from his belt, but she held him back. 'Stop that!' he shouted. 'I'm not going to hurt you! Stop! You'll bring the whole pub down on our heads.'

The narrow cellar windows rattled against their frames. Bottles tumbled from shelves and smashed on the dank tiles. Cecilia's hands were shackled in chains to sturdy wooden

101

beams that held the ceiling aloft. The panic on Popper's face suggested he wasn't lying. She'd bury them both.

Cecilia cooled and the ground beneath them settled. A cask of ale spattered onto the floor noisily behind her. 'Waste of good beer,' Popper grumbled.

Remove this thing from my face, traitor.

'No.'

She focused once more and the tiles split under his feet. A window shattered inwards. 'Very well! Stop!' Her captor crossed to her and unfastened the scold's bridle – one-handed, to keep the dagger at her eye level. The gag clattered to the floor. She spat out whatever they'd filled her mouth with and saw a sprig of rosemary unfurl in her saliva. Curious. They must not have been able to source any mistletoe or rowan – far better to curtail a witch.

'Where am I?' Cecilia demanded. When he said nothing, she made him.

'Rye! You're in Rye! Our High Mage runs this place. We didn't know where else to bring you.'

'Why? And don't lie to me, Popper, or I'll twist your spine the other way.' The rosemary sedative made her eyes feel gluey, and her power imprecise, but she found she was able to cause him pain. And, reading him, fear. He was nervous, wondering when his master and friends would return. Men are pack animals when all is said and done. Wolves.

He knew he was outmatched. 'We intend to sell you back to Cromwell. He has appointed a witchfinder.'

She wondered, honestly, if she was hallucinating. 'Are you in some manner afflicted? You are witchkind! You may as well rest your neck on the block.'

'This man, they say he seeks only women.'

'You cannot possibly be so naïve.'

'You know what I be thinking? I be thinking these men don't care if a witch is a witch. They just like getting stiff on the screams of women. Strange sport if you ask me, but so be it.'

Cecilia inhaled through her nose slowly and deliberately. 'That may be so, but if there's one thing the church hates more than women, it's the poor. Think on it, Popper. Who will they believe? A rich lady or a poor man?'

'I suppose we'll soon see.'

'Let me go, Popper . . . '

Alas, footsteps, and then more footsteps, stomped down the ladder into the cellar. Her shot at escape might have slipped away while she was talking to this warlock buffoon. She craned her neck as far as it would go to see two further men enter the grimy cellar. The first was more powerful than the second. The High Priest, she assumed. He was a tall, gaunt man with thin hair and thinner skin. There was something of an eel about him.

'Why did you ungag her, for fuck's sake?'

'It didn't work,' Popper said, shamefaced.

'Don't matter. I got some *White Sorbus* off the gong farmer.'

Cecilia bristled. Her cruel Aunt Marina had force-fed her the powder as a child to keep her gifts at bay. The effects were almost instantaneous and too much could even kill her. 'Stop,' she said as the man came closer. He stopped. She could hold him back, at least temporarily.

'Dick, throttle the cunt,' the High Priest told his young companion. 'She won't be so strong-willed then.'

'Listen to me, if you turn me over to the king you sign your own death warrants. Don't you see?'

The High Priest, Roderick was his name, smiled with stumpy little teeth. 'Doubt he even knows about us warlocks. Doubt he cares. You know, across the Channel, King Francis has a "cabal" of warlocks doing his bidding. What if we offer our services to Henry, eh?'

If she was going to act, it had to be now. She couldn't enchant all three of them at once. She couldn't risk splitting the beams and burying them all.

She quieted her noisy inner voice and *listened*. She was a witch, and all of nature was at her disposal.

Roderick examined his bottle of *Sorbus*. 'Now, how does this work then? She just eat it?'

Cecilia let her mind roam, weave, through the walls, the floorboards, the pipes. Help was everywhere if you knew where to seek it.

'Listen. Can you hear them?' she asked.

The men looked to each other. 'What's she talking about?' Popper asked.

'Shut her up.'

Samuel Popper seized hold of her hair and jaw, emboldened

now that his pack had returned from the hunt. 'You're not listening . . . ' she hissed.

Roderick shushed them all. Then they heard. From within the walls; scuttling, scratching, sniffling.

'What is that?' the young one asked.

Something scuttled in a shadowy corner, sleek and fast. Just enough to snag the eye.

And then, squeaking.

'You ought to run,' Cecilia said darkly. 'You don't know where they've been.'

'Enchantress!' Roderick struck her around the face. It didn't make a difference. She had them in her grasp. 'What phantasma is this?'

'No illusion,' purred Cecilia. 'Just *rats*.'

Like a wet, brown tide, they seeped into the cellar through a flood grate. They were like a single, swollen mass. Yet more surged in through a deep crevice in the masonry. Oddly muscular they were, black eyes glinting in the scant light. They poured over each other, almost liquid. Their shrill cries grew louder as more and more answered her call.

They swarmed on the men, surrounding them. Cecilia, unafraid, felt them crawl up her skirts and onto her back. They would not attack her.

The youngest man tripped over himself, clamouring for the ladder. 'They bring plague!' he yelped, hauling himself to the safety of the pub.

'Get back here, coward!' Roderick screamed.

As rats ran up his britches, Popper shrieked, swiping at the vermin. 'Get them off me! Get them off me!' Tears coursed down his cheeks. He was hysterical, greatly afeared of vermin – as Cecilia had well known. He tripped over the split ale cask, plummeting backwards. In a second, he was engulfed by the rodents, little nails clawing over his face and beard. It was not Cecilia's fault that the rats were so hungry. She would not deny them a meal.

Cecilia relinquished her control of the beasts, instead breaking the chains from their moorings. She drew herself upright and turned to Roderick. He fumbled with the lid of his potion, kicking the rats off his boots.

'You were warned,' she told him as she snapped his feeble neck.

· ○ ◐ ● ◑ ○ ·

LADY GRACE FAIRFAX

Hever Castle - Kent

What do you think will become of us?' Grace had asked.

Anne had insisted the kitchen prepare a picnic – apparently they were all the rage in France. Grace wasn't sure how she felt about eating with flies and bees and ants swarming around them, but Anne seemed determined. They ate manchet and cheese, salted herring and cherries, and drank wine in the shade of the oaks at the boundary of the Boleyn estate. It was a balmy day and Grace was grateful to remain in the shadows, for many reasons. Their horses were tethered a few yards away, content to graze.

'You have me mistaken for a seer,' came Anne's somewhat predictable response. She smiled over her goblet.

Grace emptied her own. Between the sunshine and the plum wine, she had grown woozy, fuzzy-eyed. No doubt the drink had fortified her to even ask her question. 'It feels like we're poised at the precipice of a very steep hill. Don't you think?'

Her companion, so radiant in the golden sun, shrugged it off and popped another cherry between her lips. 'Why don't we find out.'

'Ask a seer?'

'Ask these.' Anne stood and walked to her mare.

A vivid, red-and-black butterfly landed on the rim of Grace's plate. It was soon chased away by another and away they fluttered in some sort of dance. Were they playing or flirting, she wondered. Do insects play and flirt? As she mused on this, Anne returned with a bundle of cards wrapped in purple silk. A certain mischief on her face, she spread her deck over their blanket. They were intricately decorated, quite unlike any playing card Grace had seen before.

'What are these?'

'A game. It's called tarot. The Italian girls brought them to France. There's a game of trumps, but the witches used them to understand the past . . . and predict the future.'

'How?'

'How do seers see anything? They don't see time in a straight line, do they.'

'Magic cards?' Grace couldn't keep a wry smirk off her face.

'You're very cynical for a woman who can control the weather, Grace Fairfax.'

Grace laughed. She wanted very much to kiss Anne, there and then in broad summer daylight where everyone would see.

A kiss with sunshine on their lips and skin. Grace leaned close, so close she could smell the ripe cherries on her breath. It was giddying. If this was love, she didn't see how insanity would feel any different. Anne smiled, just inches from her mouth. Grace thought, for a second, she was going to do it, only to look back to Hever, self-consciously.

Such a thing was unthinkable, of course. God put men and women in the Garden of Eden to make babies. The *Devil* made the process feel nice. At least, that's what the hypocrites inside the church walls preached from the pulpits, and why they must remain nocturnal.

'This was how we did it back in France,' Anne told her, shuffling the deck. 'Split the cards.'

Grace looked her love hard in the eye as she did so. She saw Anne was enjoying this greatly.

'Now draw three cards.'

Humouring her, Grace did so. Seers were rare and unusual witches, and she believed they could see all of time the way the Mother could. Did she think these little cards could do the same? No.

Anne crossed her legs, ridiculous dress billowing around her like a peach cloud. 'This first image tells of your past.' She turned her card and it depicted a crowned woman holding a goblet. To Grace it was the right way up, so to Anne it was upside-down.

'A queen?' Grace said. 'Is this my future or yours?'

Anne grinned. 'Very droll. The Queen of Cups. Alas, she's

reversed. A woman, perhaps you, maybe someone influential in your life. She's sad.' Anne's voice changed; she spoke softly, kindly. 'An isolated woman, a woman who was hurt. This woman was full of potential for love and compassion, but she wasn't shown these gifts or rewarded for sharing her feelings. Quite the opposite, and so she buried them deep.'

Grace fought to keep distaste from her expression. Alone, she and Anne could talk about anything, but she'd rather they didn't talk about *her*, least of all her past. Maybe it's a northern thing. *Love* is for rich people. Growing up in humble Yorkshire, her mother and father had spoken of hunger, and sickness, and how to keep three daughters alive through the barren winter. A child would starve on love alone. Love isn't very pragmatic. 'All that from this little picture?'

Anne went on. 'Turn the next one.'

Grace did so and this time, the card showed a man and a woman, naked before an angel.

A great smile lit Anne's face. 'The Lovers! Well, I think that one speaks for itself.' This time, she did lean across the blanket to kiss her.

'Anne!'

'No one but the starlings and sparrows shall see us, and they don't seem to mind.' Anne kissed her on the lips, lingering there a while. Grace was right; a kiss in the bright yellow sunshine did feel different. It was wonderful, in fact.

Pulling away from her, Grace tapped the Lovers card. 'And

this card represents the now?' Grace asked, flushed, and Anne said it did. 'I find myself more interested in the future. The part I cannot see.'

Anne flipped the final card. 'The Sun!' she announced happily. 'A very joyful card. It seems your future is bright indeed, my love. Joy, happiness and success.'

The card showed a naked infant riding a horse under a smiling sun.

'Also,' Anne said with a naughty glint in her eye. 'It's a card which can indicate impending motherhood . . . '

Now Grace guffawed. 'An immaculate conception! Well, I suppose we're probably due one; it's been fifteen hundred years or so.'

Anne looked wounded somehow. 'I think you'd be a wonderful mother.' Grace snorted again, but she went on. 'There's none in the coven I trust more. Look at the way you care for me.'

Grace stroked the palm of her hand. 'You are not a child.'

'True,' Anne said. 'But, I think, sometimes we all need caring for as if we were still as delicate as a babe. The world is hard, yet we are not. Even you, Grace Fairfax. I wonder if that's why we call Her the Mother? Because whoever, or whatever, we are, we need that tenderness. That gentleness.'

Grace wouldn't argue with that. She only wished she could allow herself to be soft for a minute. She daren't. To expose the soft parts invited only bared teeth.

The light plunged from the forest glade, and the temperature with it. Grace looked up and saw a mean blob of cloud sitting stubbornly over their sun. 'Is that your handiwork?' Anne asked, starting to pack the picnic away into the basket.

'Afraid not. I can steer it away if you wish?'

Anne shook her head. 'No. Let it be. We should return before we're missed.'

Grace looked down at the tarot cards, now in a heap on the blanket. 'Wait. Don't you want to find out what the future holds for you?'

Anne looked at them ruefully before striding towards her horse. 'My love, I suspect I already know.'

LADY GRACE FAIRFAX

Hampton Court Palace - Middlesex

The palace grew icy as Grace swept through the halls.

Jane was poised at the side of the *other* Jane. Seymour's servants were busy, moving her possessions into the queen's chambers, while the ladies fawned over the regent-in-waiting. Margery too was with the king's newest consort, presenting her with a host of lace and satin segments. Lady Seymour fingered each delicate square with giddy excitement, and Grace knew at once they were for a wedding gown.

The temperature dropped. She couldn't help it, but Grace couldn't risk a scene in front of Seymour's coterie. 'Lady Rochford? May I steal a minute of your time?'

'Ah, Lady Fairfax, you've returned. Why, you look quite dishevelled, are you well?' Jane Rochford was almost daring her to challenge her.

Grace felt her fingers curl into a fist. She had flown in on a gale, of course she was untidy. 'It is an urgent, private matter.' Seymour now looked up, distracted from her fabrics, and eyed her with suspicion. 'It concerns your late husband.'

At that, Jane's face almost cracked like glass. She swept to Grace and removed her from the chamber. 'Must we play games, Grace?' she said once they were out of earshot.

Grace was so furious, her jaw ached. 'You tell me! I cannot fathom you, Lady Rochford.'

The other woman pulled her into a recess in the hallway. 'Lower your voice, sister.'

'Shield us from prying ears, for I shall bite my tongue no longer.' Grace felt the air around them sizzle. She didn't mean to but heat seemed to pulse from her in waves. 'Was it you?'

Jane looked briefly confused. 'Was what me?'

'You know exactly what I mean. You and Anne. You were so jealous of her. With her at court, you were as much in the background as that tapestry.'

'How dare you . . . '

'I dare like this,' Grace seethed. 'The Boleyns were a tight knot, and I would know. Anne, Mary, George, their mother and father. It must have been frustrating, gazing in from the periphery. I ask again plainly; did you tell Cromwell that Anne was a witch?'

Jane went quite pink. 'Did I condemn my husband to die? Did I consign myself to financial ruin and court ridicule? Did I jeopardise my entire coven, whom I love as I do my flesh and blood?' Her eyes blazed, irises almost gold. 'It is true my husband could be unfeeling, but I loved him, and it pains me even more that you question my dedication to the coven. I may have been a disappointing wife, but I am a witch before all else. Anne and I were one in our ambitions; a witch upon the throne, and a new age of enlightenment.'

Grace broke her gaze, abashed. She saw she spoke the truth, and she stood corrected. 'Then why were you at Esher? With that infernal man?' It hadn't taken her long to get the truth out of Isabel on returning to court.

Jane sighed. 'Why not let the witchfinder hunt Cecilia for us? We only draw attention to ourselves at a time when we need to be here, making a great show of our affection for the new queen.'

'Let her rot,' Grace said. 'What do you think will happen when Cecilia is cornered as some fox? What possible reason would she have to keep our names off her tongue?'

Jane's expression, wavering, suggested she had considered this contingency, and *that* was why she'd ploughed ahead with her plans alone. 'A risk, certainly, but a calculated one. I can't imagine they'll let her live long enough to betray us. What this is about is your thirst for vengeance. Admit it: you wanted to end her with your own hand.'

She would admit no such thing. 'Have you learned naught? We cannot trust these men, not ever. Sister, you have marked us all for death.' Grace gathered her skirts and swept away, ready to take flight once more.

Grace skimmed the thickest fog she could off the Thames, and soon the streets of Bermondsey were doused in foul-smelling smog. Hidden, Grace landed amidst the mire on the banks and made her way towards the laundries.

The narrow alleyways and lanes were busy; market day. The farmers on the fields outside the city beat their sheep towards the cattle mart while carts were stocked high with chicken and pheasant. Even at this productive hour, people spilled out of the taverns, and why not? Grace was beginning to see the appeal in oblivion.

The streets were a labyrinth and she soon became lost. Where she thought the washroom was, transpired to be a button merchant and she was forced to ask an ostler for guidance. Eventually, as her fog lifted, Grace saw Agnes Drury standing too close to a bearded magistrate outside her premises. On seeing her, the witch took a step back. Grace could understand why it would be advantageous to keep the Justice of the Peace kindly.

'Not again,' Agnes sneered. 'People going to start getting the wrong idea about my establishment. Wouldn't want people thinking it was legitimate, would I?'

Her male friend made a prompt exit, and Grace waited for him to leave earshot.

'Well?' Agnes prompted her.

'I need the seer. As a matter of urgency.'

Agnes relented. 'I know. She said you'd be coming, she's a

ruddy good seer.' Grace went to enter the laundry, but Agnes blocked her path. 'Not so fast, Pretty, last time was a gratuity, but you'll get no more.'

Sighing, Grace took a coin from her purse and pressed it into Agnes's calloused palm. 'Satisfied?'

'Rarely. This way.'

Agnes walked her through the humid laundry. The linens were whitened with urine, and the odour stung her eyes, making them water. How did they stand it? The washerwomen were red-faced, weary, as they hung vast sheets up to dry. They eyed her with suspicion as she wove through their sails.

Grace wondered what her life would have been had she not had this face. It was as if she'd been plucked from some fateful apple tree as a girl, and given as a gift: from her father to her husband. What if she'd been left on the vine? Her mother had not worked outside the home, but her aunts and cousins had been dyers or spinners, with the exception, of course, of Aunt Elinor, the apothecary. Perhaps that would have been her lot. She was oddly sentimental for that life she'd never had.

It was a slender door into a world in which she'd never come to court, never met Anne. Today, it was hard to know if she welcomed the notion. Her life would have been quieter, yes, but colourless. Too early to tell if all this pain was worth it.

Agnes led her upstairs this time, above the laundry, to a claustrophobic attic space. The roof leaned over a narrow, draughty room. In the corner, the slight form of Sindony was propped up in bed. An elder witch fed her broth from a bowl, but the girl was reluctant to take it. There was an unhealthy sheen, a pallor to her face, almost greenish.

Agnes leaned closer to Grace. *Perhaps don't get too close, Duchess.*

The child was sick. 'Where are your healers?'

'Lizzy here is our best healer. She's doing all she can.'

'Don't speak over me, I beg,' Sindony said, coughing a little. 'Don't be sparing my feelings; I seen what fate befalls me.'

Grace entered the attic and took a seat by the window. Some meagre sunshine fell across the floor. 'How long will you remain?'

'I won't be goin' out surrounded by chubby grandchildren, look at it that way,' she said with a sly smile. 'But that ain't why you came to see poor Sindony Bates.'

'I have to find Cecilia de la Torre.'

'I already answered to that.'

Grace fixed the girl in a glare. 'She didn't stay still.'

'Or you weren't fast enough.' She giggled and coughed more harshly. Her nurse held a handkerchief to Sindony's face and withdrew it, flecked with red. She then raised a cup of cloudy water to the seer's lips. The water could well kill her before the consumption did.

When her nurse was still, Sindony began. Her irises were purest white. 'Hair damp with salt. Sea birds cry. The sun sets to her face.'

West? She was due west? That was surely the wrong direction if she meant to land in France or . . . *Spain.* Yes, that made sense. Cecilia would have family in Spain. She must seek passage to Spain through the Bay of Biscay. 'The coast is in sight.'

Good. That meant she hadn't gone too far. 'Thank you.'

But Sindony continued. 'There be fire. It devours. It swallows and gulps. Do not go to her, Grace Fairfax.'

She chose to ignore the warning. 'Will I find her before the witchfinder does?'

'Depends.'

'On what?'

The girl sat up straighter. 'I say again: Do not go, Lady Grace. Call off your hunt. You have pressing business in court.'

Grace guffawed. 'I have no business in court.'

The girl's pupils returned to her eyes. She looked confused. 'You is a mother?'

A curious embarrassment became her. A sense of having failed a task she hadn't even undertaken. 'You are mistaken.'

'You is, and you will. I see that clear as day.'

'And I say again, you are wrong.' Grace was surprised to find tears stinging her eyes, but she blinked them back. She *had* been pregnant, once to the best of her knowledge, at fifteen, before Robert tired of her. She'd been relieved on the day she'd bled it out, or rather had felt a sudden and specific lightness, unburdened of the growing dread. 'I have no child.'

Sindony relented. 'As you wish.'

Grace stood, preparing to leave. Only then, because she knew she would not get the opportunity twice, she asked, 'Tell me, Seer. What becomes of us?'

Sindony didn't need to ask to whom she referred. The seer briefly looked to Agnes, who loitered on the threshold. 'It's OK, tell her.'

'War, hunger, disease. Poverty and pestilence. Who should we blame for these sufferings?'

Grace shook her head, unsure. 'There's no one to blame.'

The seer looked far beyond Grace, past the wall, past London. 'Are you sure? Because *they* will blame *witches*.'

Grace shivered, despite the springtime sun. 'Who will?'

'They all will.'

+ ○ ◗ ● ◖ ○ +

LADY GRACE FAIRFAX

Hampton Court Palace - Middlesex

Court was abuzz. There was to be a great feast that night at the king's new residence. Grace accompanied Anne and Margery to a cramped haberdashery outside the palace walls. Margery duly humoured Anne as she stroked a hundred samples of lace, though Grace could tell none apart and scarcely cared for the task. Instead, she stood at the bay window, watching feeble flakes of snow idle to the cobblestones. As soon as they touched the earth, they vanished. It would not settle.

The secret was no longer a secret. Anne was the king's, and perhaps more startlingly, the king was hers. His love was plain for everyone to see, and his affections disseminated to her family, it seemed. Tonight, they would toast the promotion of both Anne's father and brother. The former was now Earl of Wiltshire *and* Earl of Ormond, while the latter was now Viscount

Rochford. Lady Jane was beside herself, already insisting that everyone referred to her by her new title. It was a fortuitous time to bear the Boleyn name.

It was hard to not feel sorry for the queen, who was now exclusively residing at The More, exiled north of the city. The reptilian cardinal, Wolsey, had failed to do the king's bidding; he had not convinced the pope to annul his marriage. Thus, he had been dismissed, stripped of his land and titles. In fact, they were now all living in his former home, far down the Thames to the west of the city. However splendid Hampton Court was, Grace found it ghoulish, like sleeping atop his freshly dug grave.

It was, and there was no other word for it, *scary* to live under a ruler who wrote the rules as he went. Divorcing a queen; deposing a cardinal; changing the church to suit his desires. It was unprecedented and unnerving. She understood why the king was so popular; the people saw his blatant disregard of the established order as an opportunity for their meagre, humdrum lives to magically improve. They were fools if they thought that. The king served only himself, always. The empire was an extension of his self.

Grace felt an unshakable unease.

Anne looked to her, annoyed. 'Lady Grace, you must cease your relentless worrying. I don't know how you say nothing, but say it so loudly.'

Margery giggled. The shop owner was flitting around upstairs, leaving them free to talk.

Grace would have continued to stay silent, but Anne urged her to say her piece. 'Nothing feels certain,' she sighed. 'You both ought sense it better than I. The very foundations we stand on seem to shift as silt.'

'Are you saying you don't trust in the king's judgement?' The question was rhetorical, and Anne smirked slightly as she said it. 'Sister, you can trust in mine. Wolsey was against us. Better for all of us he's exiled to the grim north.'

The same grim north Grace had once called home: Yorkshire.

Anne scrutinised her closely. 'I cannot read you, Grace. What is it you hide from me?'

'A woman is entitled to her secrets, my lady. Even from a queen.'

Anne admired a brick of an emerald on her finger. A gift. 'I am not yet the queen.'

And it was those thoughts Grace must occlude from her. Nothing would stop the king. He was frenzied, obsessed. *Somehow* he would find a way to cast aside Queen Catherine and wed Anne. Grace felt hot, her corset digging into her hips. She looked away from Anne once more in the hope it would place her thoughts further out of the witch's reach. This was some choice blindness. If a man can so casually besmirch one woman, he will do so again and again and again. It was his nature, as it was an adder's to bite. Anne was naïve to think she could change him.

Two tiresome hours later, and with the alterations to her

gown complete, the women left the shop. 'Where is the carriage?' Margery asked.

The horse and carriage were nowhere to be seen. Anne raised a hand to her temple. 'I cannot sense the driver. How rude.'

Grace saw they were witness to some funeral procession. 'Here is your answer.'

A steady stream of mourners filed through the narrow street, and she could only conclude the driver had moved on to allow them passage. The black parade moved slowly towards the church and graveyard, the bells tolling distantly. Grace wondered who had perished; someone very well loved – and not without wealth – judging by those who'd come to remember them. There was a dignity to them, the women poised in their veils, supporting each other down the road. They wore sprigs of rosemary in their hats, for remembrance.

'Come,' Anne said suddenly. 'There is much to be done before tonight. The driver cannot be far.'

She hoisted up the hem of her cape and started down the street. Grace wondered if they should wait for the funeral party to finish, but she supposed they were bound in the opposite direction. They had only walked a few yards when Grace became aware of a certain scrutiny. If Grace was minded of the stares and sideways glances, then the enchantresses must be too.

Anne pulled the cowl of her cape further over her face, but this only seemed to draw further attention to her.

That's her, Grace heard someone within the procession

mutter. Further down the lane, the cortège drew to a halt – for why, Grace couldn't say – but this only meant the rumblings spread amongst the crowd like beads on a chain. *The Boleyn woman . . .*

Margery looked over her shoulder a little nervously.

Let us not dally, Anne told them directly.

Grace, even without the gift of voice, sensed it. A low mood. A distaste in their audience. Most notably from the women. The way they *looked* at Anne, as if she were covered in boils and pustules. The revulsion. For while the king was popular, so was the queen.

The king's mistress.

Were they safe here? The mourners vastly outnumbered them. They wouldn't try anything, would they? Grace felt small and oddly naked despite her cape and robes.

The king's whore, someone said, and Anne froze. 'Treason,' she said aloud.

'My lady,' Grace said, her voice low and deep. 'Keep going.' By now, she could see the carriage and the driver just around the bend, discreetly waiting.

'It ain't treason if you ain't a queen,' a ruddy woman laughed. A chuckle spread amongst the mourners.

'Why don't you fuck off back to France?' said another woman.

'You ain't no queen of ours, whore,' this woman's husband added. He would regret that comment. No sooner had he spat it, he doubled over in pain, as if he'd been stabbed in the gut.

Under her cloak, Anne's eyes were jet black. The hapless

man now clutched his chest in agony, gasping to draw breath. After a horrid second where they thought he was japing, mourners now flocked to him, panicked. *Terrance*, his wife called to him, *Terrance, what ails you?*

'Anne, I beg.' Grace leaned closer. 'Stop.'

Anne did not stop. Her jaw clenched tighter. She intended to stop his heart.

'Witch!' a voice in the crowd gasped. Grace looked over and saw a pale, crooked finger jabbed in their direction.

Grace took hold of Anne's shoulders. 'Now!' she commanded. 'We leave.'

'Her eyes!' the same woman cried. 'Look at her eyes!'

Enough. The December sky was already low and full, frozen. It took almost nothing on Grace's part to whirl the clouds overhead, to force them to release their icy load. A blizzard curled in around them. Bitter, howling winds buffeted the funeral march and many ran for cover.

Anne's hold on the hapless Terrance was broken. He looked clammy, and confused, and unsteady on his feet, but his wife gathered him, and led him towards the shelter of the Ram Inn on the corner. Even Grace felt the teeth of the wind on her face. A hand slipped into hers: Anne, trying to stay upright against the squall. Grace gripped her tight, hardly able to see through the storm.

As it blew up, down and straight, thick snow soon drifted up against the walls, painting the town white. It seemed to cast a blanket over the scene, some conjurer's trick, and within a minute the street was almost empty of everyone except them. Cries faded into the distance, leaving a perfect winter tableau with them alone at its centre. The church bells continued their lament.

'I confounded them,' Margery added. 'They won't remember much except the snow.'

Anne had the decency to look ashamed, not a style she sported often. 'Sisters, I can only apologise. I don't know what possessed me so.'

Grace did, for she had seen these tantrums before, and they were becoming more frequent. Nonetheless, she said nothing as they hurried to their waiting carriage.

If Anne was perturbed by the events on the marketplace, she didn't show it at the feast. Not one bit. Her smile was radiant, and her laughter quite contagious. They – she and the king and various Boleyns and Howards – gorged on swan and hog, pottage, and custards for dessert. A river of wine and ale flowed from the cellars to the Great Hall until the tables were cleared for dancing and music. It was an undeniably spectacular venue, as vast as any cathedral, with the king's priceless tapestries – woven with gold, no less – adorning the walls. The harpist and the citole player were given no time to rest and the king joined them on recorder, showing off as ever. In fairness, he wasn't unskilled as a musician, and Grace found it preferable to hearing his voice.

She could not feign enthusiasm for the celebration. While she was pleased Robert had not made the journey down from Yorkshire – he had gout – she was too shaken from the ugly confrontation in the marketplace to have fun. They had been seconds from disaster. Couldn't Anne see that?

Anne danced with her father, laughing, gay and delightful. She was the sun, and everyone else here whirled around her like little planets.

With the king present, and drunk, everyone was sloppy smiles, but outside of court, those commoners told a different story. Anne was not safe on either side of these walls, and all Grace could do was look on, impotent. She felt her counsel was worth less and less these days. It was all she could do to not sulk. What a bind. Even now, she wanted to be Anne's favourite – but no one likes a sulker.

Did Robert have gout? Really? The ever-present cloud of rebellion grew darker over the north. Would she be summoned home? Grace exhaled through her nose. No. She would die first. She was not going back. She had made her resolve many years ago.

Anne wove through the masses, batting off stray compliments, and Grace realised she was coming for her. She looked extraordinary in midnight-blue velvet and a pearl choker at her throat. 'Lady Fairfax! You must dance, I command it!'

'Forgive me, my lady. I think I am to retire.'

Anne took her hand. 'Nonsense, we are nocturnal, you and I.'

Grace pulled back her hand. 'I'm going to bed.'

Anne looked as though she was going to argue but decided against making a scene. 'Very well,' she said, her expression steely. 'I bid you fair dreams.' She turned curtly and returned to the king's side. He welcomed her back hungrily. The man was famished.

The smoke from Grace's bedside candle still lingered when she heard the door to her chamber open with a creak. Light from the hallway briefly filled her eyes, enough to see Anne slip inside. She carried with her a lantern. Grace could distantly hear the hurdy-gurdy, so knew the party had not yet concluded. Grace rolled over, shying away from the light.

'I came to apologise,' Anne said softly. Grace said nothing, but heard her fumble with her gown and corset. After what felt like forever, Grace felt a warm body slide into bed alongside her. 'Can I sleep here tonight?'

'If you wish.'

'It is my wish. My new chambers are cold and vast and lonely.'

'I'm quite sure the king would welcome your company.' Grace could not hide the bitterness. Not even slightly.

Now Anne was quiet a moment.

'How do you stand him?' Grace said very quietly. Her pillow absorbed her tears.

'Grace, listen to me. The king, the coven, is my work. *You* are my fate. We will not be changed, come what may.'

Grace felt hands reach past her hips and tease up the hem of her nightgown. Anne's lips brushed against her ear. 'Can I show you some of the things I learned in France?'

'About men?' Delicate fingers traced upwards the soft skin inside her thighs as her legs parted. Grace felt some tide swell inside her.

'About *pleasure*.'

LADY CECILIA DE LA TORRE

The *Folentyne* - somewhere in the English Channel

Below deck, Cecilia was tucked into a dark corner, a spider, watching the men be men in the way that men are when there are no ladies around. They belched, and guffed, and laughed, they touched themselves and scratched themselves, and joked, but mostly they worked because the time went faster that way. Under the racket, they were melancholy. They missed home, they missed women, and the softer men they could be with them. They worked hard to shield this sadness from each other.

Remaining invisible was draining, leeched all of her energy, but out here on the sea there was a well she could draw from. The oceans were an abundant source of power, and with them close by, Cecilia felt almost infinite.

It was a short voyage from Dover to Southampton. It was a small cargo ship, two decks, a forward and a main mast. There was only a half-hearted breeze behind them, but they should arrive well before nightfall. From there she would establish which ships were bound for Italy and the safety of the convents.

The Rye warlocks had not caught up with her since she'd fled the Mermaid Inn. She had no notion of the clan's numbers. Nonetheless, she'd moved as a ghost since, hiding herself from passers-by, stealing food and water only when she felt hollow and sick. She was exhausted and filthy. This stinking cargo vessel was only marginally worse than her own odour.

She was too tired to dwell on regret, on whether she'd make the same choices a second time.

The ship suddenly pitched, cranking her from her pensiveness. The crates Cecilia was hiding behind toppled backwards, shattering against the back wall. She ducked out of the way as dozens of cabbages rumbled across the cabin floor. The sailors too took hold of beams to steady themselves. They looked to one another, just as confused as she was.

'What was that?' someone called up the ladders onto the deck.

'Storm front blowing in!' a voice hollered back.

'All hands on deck!' another yelled.

The motley crewmen sprang to action, heading upwards. Cecilia pressed herself tight against the wall as the vessel now seemed to keel, the vegetables rolling sideways over the planks.

When they'd left Dover there'd scarcely been a cloud in the

sky. Cecilia knew. A familiar sensation of resignation, almost a blissful surrender in her mind. It was over. No need left to fight. They had found her.

The sudden lurching of the boat, the uncertainty of her legs, made her feel acutely unwell, but she fought the urge to vomit. Instead, she used the rough walls to guide herself to the ladder. Concentrating on her gifts, she levitated herself onto the deck.

The second she emerged into daylight, she was hit by a bitter squall that almost knocked her backwards onto her rear. Cecilia gripped the ship's rail to stay upright. Rain, sharp as pins, clawed her cheeks as she squinted to the skies. A black rose unfurled above them; furious cloud turning day to night.

'Steady the mast!' the captain cried into the storm. It was futile, the canvas mainsail tore down the centre like paper.

Stop this, Cecilia demanded of the sky.

The *Folentyne* started to careen perilously, a great tongue of a wave sloshing over the side. A young deckhand, a boy, was swept onto his back, swilled past where Cecilia hid. Cecilia could hardly see through the wall of rain but did everything she could to steady the vessel. At the same time, she knew it was useless. For Cecilia knew the name of her hunter.

And she intended to capsize them.

I implore you, Grace. These men are innocent.

No man is innocent. A single reply filled her mind.

And then she saw her, far above. From the eye of the storm,

a pale splinter emerged. Her hair and skin were ice white, her eyes jet black. She was steady, arms wide, expression unreadable. There was no rage on her face, and that made it all the more chilling.

As the ship started to yaw, spinning as if it were at the centre of a whirlpool, Cecilia slid to her knees. *Grace, please, stop. Let me explain.*

Grace remained at the centre of her tempest, looking down in cold, unfeeling judgement. A black cape billowed around her. She was the reaper, come for her bounty. Cecilia forgot sometimes that they were not as the others. They were not women, or ladies, or girls. They were something primeval, something fundamental, as unforgiving as the desert sun or frozen tundra. They were witches.

A sob broke Cecilia's throat.

Here was her reckoning, and she had never loved her more.

· ○ ○ ● ○ ○ ·

LADY GRACE FAIRFAX

The *Folentyne* - somewhere in the English Channel

Far below her, the boat spiralled like some flimsy toy on a pond, ready to become driftwood. Cecilia was a dot, drenched and cowering. From up here, Grace could grasp her between her fingers and pop her like a grape. All the power of the ocean surged through her body and she felt as one with the storm. She was the storm. It was dizzying and she felt harsh, satisfied laughter scratching at her throat, trying to get out. She'd done it. She'd found her bounty. She would avenge Anne's betrayer, kill a fleet of sailors, satisfy coven law.

She could make this cyclone stronger, tear across Sussex and Surrey and London, laying waste to the king's palaces. She could eviscerate every last scorpion who'd stung at her queen. She could turn the throne into kindling and with it every rule, every trap for girls like Anne.

But then what?

She would still be gone.

Grace could turn this power inside out. She could be the blast. The last thing she'd see would be the king's face as she became the fire that devoured him.

And she'd still be gone.

Grace did not feel like fire.

She saw Cecilia, terrified, on the deck of the ship.

And Anne: laughing as they played cards and drank buttered beere at Hever; dancing at the May Day dance; forming a circle with her coven. She remembered a time she saw Anne comforting a dispirited Cecilia on a rainy night when she'd had rather too much perry; the way she'd stroked her hair, dried her tears. Anne had been her big sister.

Coven law dictated Cecilia must burn. Only now did Grace question it. For what? Cecilia would be dead, and Anne would be dead, and Grace would still feel this yawning trench at her middle. A hole so vast Cecilia's corpse couldn't hope to plug it. So why? Why anything?

Without Grace even thinking about it, the monsoon eased. Grace had lost her control of the skies around her. The *Folentyne* still leaned, her main mast snapped, but she seemed to right herself. The soaked crew were ants, swarming to regain order.

The rain and gales ceased, but the black clouds lingered. Grace summoned a swirling fog to disguise her descent. She let herself drift downwards until her feet touched the sodden planks of the vessel.

Not a single shipman seemed aware of her landing, suggesting Cecilia was conscious and uninjured and hiding them. Grace was not immune to the elements; her hair swung across her face as tangled ropes and her dress and cape were heavy with water. She strode over the deck to where Cecilia sheltered.

'Get up,' Grace demanded.

'Make it quick,' said Cecilia, her tone flat. 'But spare these men. They don't even know I'm here.'

Grace grasped the taller woman's throat and shoved her back against the wall to the fo'c'sle. 'I *ought* kill you. Witch law commands your blood. To betray a sister is death.'

Cecilia did not deny it. Her big, copper eyes bade mercy. *Then do it.*

It would take seconds. She could steer raw lightning down her arms and she'd be dead in a heartbeat. But no. Grace removed her hand. 'No,' she said. 'I want to know *why*.' On the last word, her voice failed her. She swallowed the emotion back. She would not cry. 'Tell me why.'

It felt like Cecilia was shrinking. Normally ebullient, she wilted. 'I had to, sister.'

The sea settled, and rods of sunlight pierced her clouds. 'Why?' Grace said more forcefully this time.

Now Cecilia began to cry. 'I didn't *want* to. Of course I didn't, but I couldn't see any other way.'

'You committed treason against the crown *and* your coven. Now speak, or so help me I shall burn every soul on this ship to hell.'

The seamen worked around them, oblivious to their presence on deck. Cecilia tried to take her hands, but Grace snatched them back. 'He knew, Grace. Cromwell. He knew about you . . . and her.'

Grace recoiled, her words like a slap. She blinked flaccidly a moment. 'I don't know what you mean.'

'You do.' Cecilia was, after all, a mind-reader. What was the use in pretending? What had *ever* been the use? 'If I committed treason, it was long after you had. You and the queen both.'

Now it was Grace's turn to become mute. Anything she said would only damn her further. She thought they'd been so careful, even around the coven. She felt now the most childlike shame, her head bowed, like she'd been caught in the pantry with sugar on her lips.

Cecilia looked as a feral thing: face filthy; curls knotted; eyes wild. 'You have to understand! He, or his spies, interrogated us all. He was looking for *anything*, any paltry crumb of scandal. The king wanted Anne's head, and he wasn't going to stop until he had it. But I couldn't let him have you too.'

Grace felt her heart slow to a death knell, and everything made a sudden sense. *She* had killed Anne Boleyn, not Cecilia. 'What did you tell him?'

'I said it was lies! All of it! But he wouldn't believe me. And so I told him that Anne could enchant people – but in the mundane sense – I told him she had manipulated you; that you were a sweet, innocent, northern girl.' Cecilia looked deeply ashamed.

'And he believed it, because he wanted to believe it. But, I swear to you, I never named her a witch. Never.'

Grace had always taken a certain pride in her anonymity at court, doubting Thomas Cromwell would even know her name. But far from it; she was his proof. Of witchcraft, of perversion, of whatever he wanted. For the first time, Grace felt the cold sea air crawl over her flesh.

She turned to Cecilia. 'But why? Why would you protect me and not her? She was your High Priestess. You should have given them *me*. I'm worth nothing!'

Cecilia half laughed and half cried. 'You fool, Grace Fairfax! You blind fool!'

Grace couldn't imagine what Cecilia could possibly find so hysterical.

'She had you blinded! You couldn't see her for what she really was . . . the way she treated you . . . it was so unfair, so cruel. You deserve better, so much better.'

And at last Grace did see. For she'd felt this breed of insanity too.

Cecilia had done it for love.

LADY CECILIA DE LA TORRE

The Palace of Placentia – London

The newcomer was an enigma. Cecilia had never encountered anyone quite like her before. Meg introduced her at breakfast as Lady Grace Fairfax, the wife of an important mill owner to the north. She was slender, hair white-blonde, with a curiously feline face. Her pale blue-green eyes reminded Cecilia of the lynx the men used to hunt in the mountain ranges back in Spain.

Most people are, in essence, eggs. There's a shell, often flimsy, and beneath is the truth of their spirit. Like an egg, it's often messy within, and it takes some time to find the yolk at the centre of someone, but it's always there if you care to look.

The stranger was shell all the way through. Cecilia, across the dining table, tried to read her. Grace looked her way, briefly, before looking away. Nothing; she was giving nothing away. She was refined, *ladylike* in the way they'd all been trained to the same exacting brief. Her hue was cornflower blue, an air witch. On a promising June morning, she was January skies.

She was a witch. Did she know she was a witch? Surely a woman with that much power would know something of it. Anne sat at the queen's side. Cecilia looked to her now. *The newcomer is a witch. Do you sense it?*

Anne politely dabbed her mouth on a linen and surreptitiously looked to Grace Fairfax. *So she is. A sorceress, I'd hazard. Compelling. She is the blue in a flame.*

Cecilia, an enchantress, had always been fascinated by sorceresses. Imagine having mastery of the sky and sea. Had she been gifted in that way, how she'd have punished her uncle and aunt in Tripoli. She'd have laid ruin to their villa, brought mountain and floods down on their heads, and burned their bones to dust. They would have paid for their sins.

Should I speak with her? Cecilia asked Anne.

No. Patience, child. For now, we watch and wait. We must consult also with the coven. She may be a spy.

For whom? Neither king nor queen knew of their secret meetings, but Boleyn was in charge. There had been no vote, but she undeniably led. She was born for it.

Over the days that followed, Cecilia stayed close to the new witch as she found her way around court. The palace was a maze, but Grace carried out her tasks diligently. She spoke with a funny northern twang, but only when spoken to; she was friendly but never familiar. Cecilia remained unable to read her soul in any meaningful way. She was *pleased* to be here and *glad* to serve under the queen. The way she gripped herself in was admirable, if frustrating, to a natural snooper like Cecilia.

She was elegant, even when she was away from the gaze of the men, almost aloof. Cecilia found herself intrigued. She watched her one afternoon, doing some needlework in a sunny window seat overlooking the river. Unaware Cecilia was in the doorway, Grace finished a stitch, rested the tambour frame in her lap, and turned her face to the sunshine. The woman's shoulders dropped an inch or so and she exhaled for the longest breath.

There. Just a glimpse, but Cecilia felt something real.

Freedom.

It took some bartering, but Cecilia convinced Bess Graves to switch bedchambers so that Cecilia could share with Grace. She felt it was wise to keep the witch under close surveillance, and they were both permanently at court, unlike Lady Graves. Anne backed the move.

Grace had been at court for a couple of weeks when Cecilia saw her watching her write letters to her friends in France. It was night, and Cecilia had been hunched over a single candle so as to not wake her new companion. 'Is it difficult?' Grace asked.

Cecilia rested her quill and turned in her seat. 'What?'

'Writing. I was never taught.' It sounded like a confession, but it didn't carry any shame. Most girls weren't instructed in reading or writing. What was the point? Cecilia had been forced to, first by her cruel aunt to earn her keep, and then by circumstance. She'd travelled so far; it was the only link she had to the coven back in Paris.

'Do you read?' Cecilia asked.

'A little,' Grace replied. 'I had an aunt. An apothecary. She showed me how to identify ingredients in jars.'

Cecilia decided against probing the fact Grace's aunt was an apothecary. If that was true, that meant she was almost certainly a witch too. 'Come here. I'll show you.'

Grace pushed back her bedcovers and wrapped a shawl over her nightdress. It was a warm enough night, and the palace was peaceful. Grace drew a second chair over to the little writing desk under the window. 'You have lovely penmanship.'

'Thank you. That I mostly taught myself. The girls in France were so much better than I was, but that's how it's done, I suppose. You watch, and you copy, and you learn.' Grace said nothing but nodded in the gloom. 'You already know that every letter has a sound?'

And so it began; each night, before bed, Cecilia would write a few words. Grace would read them and then copy them. If there was a better way to teach the art, Cecilia didn't know it.

Although Grace's mental portcullis remained resolute, Cecilia determined one thing: Grace was *determined*. She had resolved to learn this skill and she would. Even after the longest day in court, even if there had been a celebration or feast, Grace picked up a quill.

'You learn quickly,' Cecilia said one night, maybe a month after Grace had arrived at court.

'I have had to,' Grace muttered as the nib scratched over her parchment. 'To be clever is to survive.'

'I couldn't agree more,' Cecilia said. They were shoulder to shoulder at the tiny desk. Their skin pressed together, and Grace didn't attempt to put space between them. Did she desire the company of women? If only Cecilia could read her, then she would know. The wants of Grace Fairfax were buried treasure, and they were buried deeply.

That night, that very night, Cecilia awoke to witchcraft. She could feel it in the stale air of their chamber. Her eyes struggled against the thickest black, but she was dimly aware of Grace sitting upright in her bed. The woman looked confused, almost lost in trance. Just as Cecilia was about to speak, to ask if she was well, Grace swung her legs off the cot and crept towards the door.

Cecilia sensed confusion, excitement and exhilaration in her. Elsewhere, Cecilia felt Anne's unmistakable aura: swirling, molten amber. She couldn't hear what Anne was saying, but her whisper was in the air. She was siren-calling to Grace, and Grace alone. The time to summon the new witch, to reveal themselves, had come.

It took Cecilia a moment to identify the awful ache in her chest as disappointment. She knew when she was beaten.

◦ ○ ◑ ● ◐ ○ ◦

LADY GRACE FAIRFAX

The *Folentyne* – somewhere in the English Channel

With only one sail, the ship was crawling towards Southampton, but they were at least heading in the right direction. Grace summoned a gentle wind to aid their voyage. It was the least she could do, considering the damage she'd done. Now she was calm, Grace felt ridiculous. She could have killed someone – many someones – people with lives and friends and children. Who was she to snuff out a light so casually? A dreadful symptom of her time around the king: life and death had become trivial.

The witches sought the solace of the captain's cabin. Cecilia ensured he wouldn't disturb them. The cramped quarters were far from luxurious, but it was private.

Grace would not mock or belittle Cecilia's feelings, but nor would she excuse her actions. There was a narrow, grimy window in the cabin. Grace looked out over the horizon and saw through the sea fret a vague notion of the craggy British coastline.

'Sister, I cannot forgive what you did.'

'I had no choice.'

Grace looked at her. 'You did. You should have given them me,' she said it without histrionics. 'I would have thought that was obvious. As a coven we had aims. Anne was more valuable than I was, any fool can see that.'

Cecilia came to her side, sitting next to her on a narrow bench seat. 'That isn't true.'

'Yes it is! She was the *queen*. She was everything we were working towards. A new age for women like us.'

Cecilia pulled at her wrists until Grace faced her. 'How can you all be so blind? We had nothing!' she raged. 'Anne was a *toy* the king grew bored of. Don't you see? We never had any real power, only what he allowed her. One way or another, he'd have removed Anne because she didn't fulfil his needs any more. My word alone was scant evidence, little more than tittle-tattle, and yet they were only too willing to believe it. What I did saved the rest of us.'

Grace pulled her hands free and swept across the cabin. 'Fool! You did nothing of the sort! Right now the king's personal witchfinder hunts you like a wounded deer. You and Jane have brought ruination to us. This will be the end of the coven. The game is over, and we lost.'

Crestfallen, Cecilia looked to her empty palms. 'I . . . I thought it would be the end of things, and that we . . . '

'And that *we* what?' Grace put her hands on her hips. Her dress was still sodden and filthy. Cecilia could only look to her, her bottom lip trembling. 'Don't. We, above all others, cannot be slaves to our hearts. Such thoughts lead us astray.'

'Why can't we?' Cecilia insisted, speaking with renewed purpose. 'All of this, *everything*, is because of the idle whims of some man or another. Is it our lot to cater to their desires and never answer to our own?'

'Yes!' Grace now shouted, waving her open hands in Cecilia's face. 'That *is* our lot in this unjust world. Hadn't you noticed?'

Cecilia rose, braver. 'I have spent *years* trying to understand you, Grace Fairfax. You cannot possibly be as cold as you seem. It is all lies. You are a lie. I think you were so hurt, so young, that you built a fortress of yourself. But somewhere inside of you, there is a woman, a woman who loved.' She drew a breath before going on, more softly. 'You did love Anne. You loved her greatly. Why deny it? Everything you have done was for her, so you and I are equally guilty of acting out of selfish, stupid, exquisite love.'

Grace flinched from the barrage of words. To talk about loving a woman felt at once both so unnatural and so correct. She felt naked, and unconsciously pulled her wet cloak across her front. Yes, it was true. Her choices, from the age of eight, had been fight or die. For the fight she had needed the thickest armour. She was still here, still fighting, but, goodness, the skin she wore was heavy, and she was tired. 'Be that as it may, Anne is dead, and with her goes my purpose.'

'That isn't true—'

'Do not presume to tell me how to feel, sister. I am sorry, truly, that I never understood the extent of your affection for me, and I am sorry if I caused you pain.'

'You did not—'

Grace ploughed on. 'But while we are sisters, that is the manner in which I love you.'

She imagined something shattering within Cecilia; her heart a sad little bauble hanging in her chest. Her whole face sagged with disappointment, but what had she expected? 'What will you do with me?'

Grace exhaled. The thirst for blood was all gone. She felt only sadness, in that she felt nothing at all. 'Just go. Go far away. I shall tell them you are dead.' Perhaps, if Cecilia truly felt as strongly for her as she claimed, this was punishment enough. 'If I have one thing left in this sorry world, it seems, it's my mercy.'

'But what of the witchfinder?'

Grace looked out of the window and saw the silhouette of Southampton port take shape on the horizon. She supposed she had a decision to make; the same one as every other day: *fight or die.*

THEN – 10 JANUARY 1534

· ○ ◐ ● ◑ ○ ·

LADY GRACE FAIRFAX

Hatfield House - Hertfordshire

Grace could avoid her no longer. She had been formally summoned by the queen. Looking out of her carriage window, she saw a handsome redbrick house with a finely pruned privet maze to the front. The sky was low and grey, frost still sparking on the tiled roof.

Grace had reconciled herself to a singular pain, of which she had learned much this last year. She thought she'd been sad in Yorkshire in her marital home, but this was different. There, she'd had a constant yearning, a hunger to flee. Here, there was a sore conundrum, wanting to be close to Anne, but having the feeling press down like a heel to her chest.

This was going to hurt.

Grace thanked her rider and made her way into the house. Anne's rather more impressive carriage was already at the stables, and the flag billowed at full mast to recognise the presence of the queen consort.

A fleet of servants welcomed Grace into the home and took her cape. A nanny showed her to the princess's chamber. A hearty fire rumbled in the hearth, and it took Grace a moment to locate Anne. She cradled the baby in her arms at the window, shielded by an array of ladies. Anne's hair was down, and the baby played with it. She couldn't look away from the child as she cooed and kissed her soft ginger head.

Grace was surprised to see her so . . . unassuming. Always full of surprises, even now.

She politely cleared her throat, and Anne finally looked away from the baby. 'Lady Fairfax, I'm so pleased you could join us.' She cast a glance across her audience. 'Please, if we could have the room a moment.' A nanny reached for the child. 'No, leave Elizabeth with me.'

Grace hung back as her ladies filed out of the grand bed-chamber.

'I get so little time with her,' Anne stated dreamily. She rocked the infant in her arms as she rose to greet her. Now alone, she went to kiss Grace, but Grace curtsied out of her path.

'Your Highness.'

'Grace, please. It's us. Nothing's changed.'

'Forgive me, Your Highness, but I rather think it has.'

'Nonsense!' Anne said, jovial. She offered Princess Elizabeth to her. 'Here; would you care to hold her?'

Grace recoiled as if she were being handed a live wild boar. 'I think not.'

Now Anne laughed, a proper belly laugh, and the gay noise alone tugged Grace in both directions. 'Oh Grace, you are silly! She is just a baby, and I am still just a woman. That's what they don't tell you before you become queen . . . nothing really happens. I was expecting to perhaps glow, but alas.'

Grace moved to the clouded windows, moist with dew. 'Did you not feel the Holy Spirit enter you as the crown touched your head?'

Anne settled the princess in her crib and joined Grace. She took her hand. It was warm and soft and real. Grace felt as if she were coming down to earth after months of floating in thin air, scarcely interacting with reality. 'Grace. Please.' Anne looked up at her from the window seat, eyes wide with sorrow. 'We knew it would come to pass sooner or later. This was the plan, was it not?'

Grace sighed and joined her on the bench. 'I have missed you,' she said. A confessional.

Anne looked to the heavens. 'Oh my dear Grace, if only you knew how I longed for your company. For your touch.' She added quietly, 'This last year has felt like falling; tumbling down and down ever faster.'

What would happen when she hit the ground? Grace kept the thought as hidden as she could behind her lingering resentments. She had not yet healed from the skewer of being told of their secret nuptials, after the fact. She and the king had simply returned to court from Dover, and Anne had delivered the news so casually, like an insouciant dagger betwixt her ribs. *It is done*, she had said as you would tell a friend a pie was ready.

And, because this was what the coven had always wanted – a witch on the throne – Grace could only feign satisfaction as her beloved married an ogre. Yes, yes, yes, she had a husband of course, but he was three hundred miles away and a husband in name alone. Anne knew: Grace loved only her. The same could not be said of Anne.

How could she love such opposites? Grace found it unfathomable. The question, the doubt, was what haunted Grace as she lay alone in bed each night. For her, there was no other. Before her now was physical proof that for Anne, there was someone else in her bed. This tiny, hateful, squirming child was borne of *him*.

Scarcely had she recovered from the wedding when the news of Anne's quickening arrived, rippling through court like a murmuration of sparrows. Then the coronation, then the birth; all that in the space of ten breathless months.

Ten months in which Grace had felt herself slipping further and further away from Anne. The queen. And, worse, she sensed Anne was enjoying her position.

'Grace, I beg,' Anne said, reading her. 'Worry not. I am of the same mind. You and the coven, always . . . ' Anne pressed her forehead against Grace's and she was granted her first moment's peace in over a year. The longest year. 'Only now, there's Elizabeth as well.'

And the moment ended as soon as it started. Anne stood and almost danced to the side of the crib, draping herself over the side to stroke the child's head. 'Isn't she beautiful?'

Grace begrudgingly joined her at the cot. In fairness, the baby was one of the sweeter she'd seen; placid and cherubic. She wore a fabulous gown of silk and lace. 'How old is she now?' that was a question she'd heard women ask mothers at such occasions.

'Just five months, can you believe it?' Anne gazed at the princess, and Grace felt the most absurd jealousy, craving the nights when she'd looked to *her* with such adoration. 'I lied, Grace.'

'You lied?'

Anne nodded, running a thumb over the baby's plump cheek. 'When I said I hadn't changed. I have. How could I not?' She admired the little girl a moment. 'I know I'm supposed to be all-powerful, as both queen and high priestess, but I stand before you humbled.'

'How so?'

She never once took her eyes off the babe. 'It is a great leveller, birth. In those moments; delirious on my back, legs aloft; bent over in agony; strange hands pawing and dabbing at my flesh, I wasn't anything special. I was just one more beast of burden, birthing live young. I may as well have been a heifer. Having been through all that, it's impossible to think of myself as majestic. I am queen, I am witch, and now, mother.'

Why did that word feel like such a weapon? Grace would never have children, and Anne's words went to exclude her somehow. How could she *possibly* understand Anne any longer, when she hadn't been through this feminine rite? The one coven she wasn't invited to join. Alone, that was what Grace felt. Cold, and alone.

'No, you mustn't,' Anne said.

'Please refrain from reading my thoughts,' Grace said, striding away from her.

'You . . . you are most disquieted, my love, I cannot help it.' Anne approached her from behind and slid her arms around her waist. Grace felt her chin rest on her shoulder. 'I will be returning to court more permanently. There is much to be done and I have promised my king a little brother for Elizabeth.'

Grace said nothing, but stroked Anne's hand where it sat on her stomach.

'There will be more time for us.'

'What of the princess?'

'She will remain here.'

'Why?' Grace understood a lady of Anne's standing wouldn't be expected to raise the child herself, but for her to be kept so far from court seemed unusual.

Anne sighed, frustrated. She drew herself tall and she was the version of Anne that Grace recognised. 'My love, I harbour great worries. About Mary and her mother. The Catholics despise me. My darling Elizabeth is safer here, away from it all. And the air is sweeter here, do you not think?'

Grace felt her heart sink as she said it, but say it she must. 'Then you must remain here also,' Grace said.

Since that fateful day in Hampton with the angry mob, the public mood remained lukewarm at best. Even Grace had been stunned at the coronation. It was designed to be as glorious as any heavenly ascension, but as the veiled Anne had been paraded through the streets of London in her gleaming golden litter, the applause had been limp; the onlookers curious more than awed.

'A queen's place is at the side of her king.'

Grace's expression let Anne know exactly what she thought of that. 'I want you safe,' she asserted. 'The coven can only do so much without exposing ourselves.'

Anne kissed Grace swiftly on her lips before her expression hardened. 'I am *queen*, Grace. Those traitors – Fisher, More, Catherine, Mary, all of them – they will accept me as their one true monarch or they will be tried and executed for treason.' Anne then smiled brightly. 'That's how it goes, isn't it?'

Grace flinched, but Anne did not see, already reaching into the crib to lift the baby up once more.

'Please, Grace, hold her. For me? She won't bite. She can't yet!'

Grace allowed Anne to hand her the Princess Elizabeth; she understood Anne well enough to know she would get her way in the end. Poor little thing, what a cursed family to be born into.

✦ ○ ◑ ● ◐ ○ ✦

LADY GRACE FAIRFAX

The Port of Southampton - Hampshire

Hidden by magics, Grace and Cecilia disembarked the *Folen-tyne* as the weary crewman carried crates of cargo down the gangplank to the waiting docks. There was much interest in the ship that had weathered the freak storms and hobbled into port. A crowd gathered, coming to gawp at the damage. The witches spoke as the men went about their business. 'Keep us occluded until we're into the town,' Grace told her. 'No one knows us here, and we can disguise ourselves as commoners.'

'Any of these ships could be bound for the continent.'

Already evening was setting in, and soon night and the tides would be against them. Nothing would set sail tonight. 'We shall seek an inn or lodgings for the night,' Grace told her.

A number of taverns and brothels overlooked the dock, for obvious reasons. Grace reasoned one of them had to be less salubrious for visiting clergy. There would be somewhere safe enough for them to seek sanctuary for a night. It might be wise for Cecilia to let them see her as a man. Two women travelling alone would attract suspicion.

I'd already thought the same, Cecilia told her.

Grace deduced that they had a considerable head start on Ambrose Fulke and his hounds. *They* didn't have the benefit of a soothsayer to guide their search.

The witches climbed the slick, moss-covered sea steps away from the docks, towards the welcoming lanterns in the windows on the quay. 'Where will you go?' Cecilia asked her. 'Will you come with me?'

'No,' Grace said. She felt it wise not to give Cecilia false hope. Grace knew only too well how poisonous that substance could be.

Cecilia persisted, somewhat out of breath. The harbour steps were laborious. 'It is said there is an island, somewhere in the Aegean Sea, an island of women. Of women like *us*.'

The legend of Aeaea. It was a nice story, but Grace feared that was all it was. What witch wouldn't be seduced by the notion of a place where she could live openly, revel in her talents free from persecution or ridicule? It was too good to be real, because Grace had seen how relentlessly cruel the world really was.

'You'll spend forever looking for Aeaea, Cecilia. If I were so minded, I'd settle for a haven in Spain or Italy. I'll tell the coven I killed you myself and face the consequences.' Grace reached for Cecilia's chest and tugged the locket from around her neck. 'For proof.'

'And what then? You'll serve the new queen?'

'I cannot. It would be too painful. And she's a dullard.'

'Then where?'

Grace paused. Once she said this aloud there was no going back. Her words had a witness. 'I will go to the north. Not to my husband. Let him think I died. I shall find a small, warm, secretive nook in the dark of the woods. A cottage or den or some such. I'll live alone. Children will fear me. I will be their witch.'

Cecilia grasped her hand. 'No. Grace. Those women . . . those women will be the first to . . . '

'To be rounded up and drowned? I expect so. I look forward to the day they try.'

A shrill wind cut across the cobbles of the quay. Grace was still damp from earlier, and was keen to be out of the wet clothes. With all the ships in port for the night, the taverns that lined the quay were in high spirits; music and warmth radiated from within. It was a dilemma: to go somewhere quiet away from prying eyes, or to get lost in a thrum somewhere.

As they passed the closest tavern – the noisiest – Grace asked Cecilia, 'Do you sense danger?'

Cecilia concentrated. 'Nothing out of the ordinary. Men; some running away, some running towards.'

'Let us keep going.' Eventually, the quay darkened and they

came to a large lodging house. A single candle glimmered in a downstairs window. 'Here, this looks anonymous enough.'

Grace looked to Cecilia and saw she looked like a tall, slender man; bald with beady eyes. The sort of face no one would think about twice. Grace moved closer to her, acting as this man's wife. She hoped Cecilia's illusion also stretched to making her resemble something that hadn't crawled out of the ocean.

A weary-looking woman, her cheeks hollow, greeted them with a lantern. 'You looking for beds?'

They said they were, and while she regarded them with suspicion, she didn't ask questions, not least as Grace handed her twice the amount of coin she required.

Mrs Hardy, the landlady, took a key from a drawer and led them up a tight, haphazard staircase, her candle lighting their path. The lodging house was quite the labyrinth, the claustrophobic corridors twisting and turning, with landings off landings and chambers tucked away in furtive alcoves. They eventually came to the second storey. A window in the corridor looked out over the Channel for miles.

There was a curious aroma about the place; not wholly unpleasant, but it caught at the back of Grace's throat. She prayed the rooms were at least clean and warm. 'Mrs Hardy, could we perhaps trouble you for some warm water and cloths to . . . ?'

But Mrs Hardy's face wrinkled into a frown. She stared at Cecilia. 'Who did you say you were?'

'We're the Smiths, from London,' Cecilia said, reaffirming her enchantment.

The woman's expression hardened further. 'Your face . . . what manner of trickery is this?' Hardy backed away down the hallway, fearful.

'There is nothing to concern yourself with . . . you must now show us to our room.' Cecilia spoke with authority, taking a step towards her.

Something was badly wrong. Instinctively, Grace backed down the corridor into the shadows. Was Hardy a witch? She should not be able to defy Cecilia's will.

'Demon!' Hardy wailed. 'Your face! Your face changes. Witch! I name thee witch!'

'Cease this!' Cecilia cried, but Hardy ran.

Grace wasn't aware of the presence behind her on the stairs until it was too late. A wraith-like figure in a peaked hat drifted towards them, lantern aloft. The way the light hit his skeletal face it was as if Death himself stalked towards her.

'Stay where you are, whore.'

Fulke. How? How had he . . . ?

There wasn't time to dwell on it. Grace, acting intuitively, attempted to summon the winds, or even lightning. She felt a familiar crackle around her fingers, but nothing more. She was powerless.

'Submit, devil women,' he said, too calmly. 'Your witchery shan't harm us.'

Grace retreated, colliding with Cecilia in the darkness. 'How can this be?' Cecilia gasped.

Footsteps thundered upstairs towards them in the other direction. There must be a back staircase – Hardy had fled that way – and now many feet hurried their way.

'*White Sorbus*,' Fulke said, his expression triumphant. 'A balm to your dark magics, I believe. To defeat succubi, one must learn the secrets of their bedevilment.'

'How did you find us?' Grace rasped, body pressed against Cecilia tightly.

'The same way you found each other.'

Jane Rochford. She too must have visited the seer. Agnes Drury's only loyalty was to silver and gold. Jane had sold Cecilia to the witchfinder, and they had walked willingly into a rat trap.

'Once I knew you were destined for this shore, I had my men in every guesthouse along the quay, consecrating them all,' Fulke said. 'I am surprised to find you conspiring, Lady Fairfax, although perhaps I should have expected it. The devil doth tempt the feeble-minded girls.'

The *Sorbus* had rendered her useless. She tried to chill the air, but couldn't focus. She felt a creep in her marrow. For the first time in her life, she felt *weak*, a glimpse perhaps of every other girl cursed to walk this earth.

'Let us take our leave,' Cecilia said. 'We mean you no harm.'

He advanced towards them. 'What honour before God would I have left if I were to show mercy? I am His sword on earth and must crusade in His name. No, Jesus faced Satan in the wilderness with fortitude and now I must do the same.'

With no other recourse she could conjure, Grace grasped Cecilia. 'Run.'

One of Fulke's men reached the top of the back stairs, blocking their exit. That left only upwards. Grace hoisted up her skirts and charged to the third floor of the property. Up here, the passageway was narrower still, the ceiling not much higher than her crown. She tried door after door, but they were all locked.

'Here!' Cecilia yelled. With what limited power she had, Cecilia held her hand over a lock until Grace heard it snap.

Fulke, and three other men, surged towards them. 'In!' Grace cried as Cecilia shoved the door open.

Once inside, Grace pressed it shut with her shoulder. 'Quickly! Barricade the door!'

The air in the poky chamber didn't feel so gluey, and she wondered if they had only scattered the poison throughout the halls. Cecilia dragged a feeble bedframe over and threw it against the wall. 'That won't be enough!'

Both women pressed their bodies against the timber until the head of an axe splintered the wood. Cecilia cried out.

'Can you hex them?' Grace winced.

'I cannot! I feel drunk!'

Grace felt time slipping away, just as she had on the day of the execution. Had Anne known, the way she knew now, that those were her final moments? Grace looked around the room for anything, any shred of redemption. Cecilia screamed again as a gloved arm punched through the door. 'Grace!'

And then she saw it. The room was sparsely furnished but had a small fireplace. On the hearth was a candle and, next to that was a tinderbox. It just might be enough.

She turned to Cecilia. 'Go.'

'What?'

'The window. Take flight.'

'I cannot . . . my gifts are diminished, I'll fall.'

'You will not. Once outside, you'll be free of this miasma. Now go!'

'What about you? You can fly too! Come with me!'

Through the gash in the door, she saw Fulke's unblinking, bloodshot eye peering in. Is that how she'd looked as she'd descended on the *Folentyne*? Rabid, bloodthirsty? Grace shook her head. 'I can stop them.'

'But—'

'These men will not stop unless I stop them. Not just for you, but for all of us. He knows too much. Please, Cecilia, just go!'

She darted to the spindly desk chair and shattered what glass was in the narrow attic window. Cecilia let go of the door and ran to the window. 'Find me.'

Even after everything, like the bottom of Pandora's box, the last thing left was hope in her eyes. The poor girl would soon learn. 'Get to a ship. Go. You shan't be hunted again.'

Cecilia had time only for the briefest final glance at Grace, and it was filled with regret and longing. Too late, for Grace was already at the fireplace, grasping the little tinderbox. If there was any justice left in the world, it would work.

The witchfinders made short work of their pathetic barricade. Fulke entered the room first and saw Cecilia drop from the windowsill. 'Go! Get after her! She is fleeing!'

Two of the men ran back to the stairs.

'Stay where you are, witch.'

Only then did he see what she possessed in her hands. Grace wasn't one for speeches. She struck the box and the flimsy spark was enough. She took hold of it and created a flame. She wrapped it around her fingers.

Come now, fire, be with me.

Fulke's eyes bulged.

As best she could with her powers so dampened, Grace let the fire be the way it so badly wanted to be. She allowed it to travel up her arms and into her hair. Her cape caught fire. Her skirts went next. Within seconds, she was a column of flame; a bonfire. Tongues licked the low ceiling. The curtains roared to life. Grace felt her skin peel, but she felt no pain. She and the fire were one.

She started towards her enemy, one foot in front of the other, arms outstretched.

Fulke went to run, tripping over his companion. He managed to stay upright. She wondered if he felt like Anne had as she'd so calmly walked onto the scaffold at the Tower of London. Did he know his time was nigh?

'Please,' he uttered as black smoke clogged the air.

She saw only fire as she embraced him. Her flaming arms pulled him close to her breast. He howled and howled; agony. The stench; the meaty fetor of cooked flesh. She said to his blackened ear, 'I am the devil thou hast made of me.'

He didn't scream for long.

NOW – 21 MAY 1536

LADY CECILIA DE LA TORRE

The Port of Southampton - Hampshire

It was so fast. The inferno swallowed it whole, as if the whole guesthouse was made of dry kindling. The skeleton of the lodgings was engulfed by a thick, spiralling plume of smoke. *Cloud* didn't do its sheer mass justice somehow.

Cecilia watched from the edge of the quay. Out here, she felt herself again, and could use her gifts unhindered. She made herself invisible.

She waited, and waited, until all her hope had gone. No one had emerged from the pyre in some time now. Little black charcoal people swarmed the perimeter, trying to stop the blaze from spreading to the neighbouring buildings. Every sailor from every tavern rushed to help, a chain of men ferrying buckets up from the docks.

Fulke had not come alone. As soon as she'd lowered herself to the ground and hidden herself from view, she'd seen his men pour from the neighbouring almshouse. Without their leader, they seemed lost and untethered. They looked young, not that that was any excuse. As they weighed up whether or not to rush into the burning building, Cecilia made their mind up for them by bringing down a charred rafter inches from where they stood.

She waited as long as she dared. No one was getting out of the fire alive now. Hardy, the housemistress, was beside herself, wailing in the arms of a drunk priest. Cecilia hoped, truly, that any paying guests had fled as the fire had started. It was still early into the night. Surely not too many would have been asleep at this hour, if any at all.

As she watched the flames lick the sky, she suppressed a swell of fury. Grace could have escaped the same way she had; of that she had no doubt. Grace had chosen to remain. She laughed, a moment of insanity. How could any woman follow Anne Boleyn? Grace had chosen death rather than live on. Fool.

The thought left a sour taste on her tongue. It could not be clearer now: It was never to be her. Grace Fairfax had never loved her, at least not in the manner Cecilia loved Grace. The hot moment passed, and she felt only sadness. And gratitude. Grace had been right in that regard: Fulke would not have stopped. Even with her powers diminished, she'd sensed his fervour. There was something broken in him that he thought God would fix.

A sea breeze ran through Cecilia's curls, and she turned to the black ocean. Somewhere, beyond the sky, there was an island of witches. She would never stop hunting for it. She started for the docks, the warmth of the fire on her back. There was much to live for.

· ○ ○ ● ○ ○ ·

LADY GRACE FAIRFAX

The Port of Southampton - Hampshire

Beyond the town's boundary wall, next to God's House Tower, there was a ditch. At the bottom, a sluice gate opened at high tide to prevent water flooding into the streets. And that was where Grace found herself when she woke. She pulled herself, naked, into the silt and sand. She was badly burned but alive. She had somehow, for the first time, controlled fire. It had claimed her skin and hair, though, and she would surely soon die from her injuries.

In the shallows, she rolled in saltwater foam. She was mercifully numb, able to cool herself. On her back, she stared up at the crescent moon; a delicious sliver. In that final moment, back at the guesthouse, she had found she was not ready for death. The desire to fight on had surprised her. A life without Anne was a mystery, but one she would solve. So much of who Grace Fairfax was had been forged in the years before she met

Boleyn. Who would she be after her, because of her? She would find out.

If she could heal. She had walked through the blaze, but could not gauge how close death was.

Her aunt, so many years ago, had told her witches were not like the regular folks. They had close communion with their true goddess, Mother Earth. Witches were not of flesh and blood alone. They were of the sea, and sky, and the grass and the air. As a sorceress, Grace knew this better than anyone.

I need you now, she told no one in particular. *Come to me. Heal me, I beg.*

Grace found she could no longer move her charred arms or legs. She could scarcely open her eyes. Spent, she felt herself sinking into the sediment; a rich blend of sand, shells, plants and fishbones. There was no such thing as *dirt* to a witch. It was all one thing in her infinite forms.

She was engulfed into the silt, the moonlight fading to blackness as her face was swallowed. Her heart rate slowed, and she ceased to breathe. Lowered, further and further, down and down again. Somehow, there was air aplenty in the spaces between the grains of sand. She was held fast, safe. She was cradled in the arms of her Mother.

· ○ ◐ ● ◑ ○ ·

LADY GRACE FAIRFAX

Hampton Court Palace - Middlesex

Grace was reading in the light of the fire in the queen's drawing room. She no longer gave mind to the letters alone; they formed their words effortlessly and she enjoyed thinking about their meaning. Many of the books she found around the palace were religious in nature, and mostly in Latin, although increasingly in English since the separation. They were love letters to God, really, another form of prayer.

Some were about witches. It seemed people liked to read about them. They were paranoid screeds, woefully inaccurate in nature; conflating witches with Satanis. It was as if they couldn't imagine a woman without any sort of freedom from a male overlord. Good girls for God; bad ones for Satan. Grace wondered if that was what truly scared these fanatical menfolk, the realisation that they simply weren't needed.

There was a crash and a clatter at the door and Grace set

aside the tome she was reading. Cecilia appeared in the doorway, flustered. 'Sister, what troubles you so?'

'You must come at once.' She lowered her voice. 'It's the queen.'

Grace followed Cecilia through the chilly halls of the palace to her bedchamber. The bedsheets were askew, and stained with a pool of red-brown blood. At once Grace knew what had happened. *Not again.*

It took her a moment to locate Anne. She was crumpled on the floor of her private chapel, hunched in prayer. Grace went to her side and spoke with a feather of a voice. 'Come back to bed. You must rest.'

'No,' Anne snarled. Grace recoiled. Never had she seen the queen so unkempt. Greasy tears stained her cheeks, and her hair flowed free.

'I'll give you privacy.' Cecilia bowed her head before leaving.

'What dark curse is this?' whispered Anne.

Grace pressed her face to Anne's. 'This is no witchcraft, my love, this is simply nature's way.'

Grace had been around women her entire life. Sometimes a baby wasn't to be.

'How much misfortune am I expected to tolerate?' Anne sobbed. She looked to her, eyes pink and raw. 'What is wrong with me, Grace?'

'Nothing! Nothing is wrong with you. Look at the princess. She's perfect, as are you.'

Her white knuckles clawed angrily at her stained skirts. 'I promised him. I promised him a boy.'

Grace felt her sympathy run dry. 'You owe him nought.' Maybe she ought not have said that, but she believed it. She was so very tired of the king's wants.

Anne leaned in close, pressing her head to Grace's bust. 'You don't understand, Grace. I must. I *must* give him his son.'

'You have given him enough.'

Anne turned. Grace had seen this a hundred times. The way the weather changed in her lover. Storms blew in even on cloudless skies. 'Silence! You know nothing! You know nothing of duty, of service.' The queen stood and hobbled to her bedchamber. 'You serve only yourself, Fairfax, you always have, a slave to your selfish desires, and yet you lecture me so blithely on marriage, on the coven.'

Grace said nothing. She also knew it was pointless to argue with her when she was like this.

Anne grabbed her cape and slung it about her shoulders. 'Oh! Hold your tongue, as you always do, but know I hear you all the same. Your judgement *reeks*, sister, but this is for you. All of this is for you.'

Grace took a breath. There was a time when she would have held her tongue. What a coward she had been. If only she'd had the strength to beg, they might not be here now. 'Tell me you did not want to be queen and I'll believe you.' Anne glowered at her but voiced nothing. Grace went on. 'You were a queen before the crown. The witch queen. Why was that not enough?'

Anne's voice was low, gravelly. 'Get your cape. We fly tonight.'

'To where?' Grace closed her eyes, waiting for the deluge to pass.

'I need real witches.'

A waxing silver moon rippled in the glistening mudflats. The spire of St Paul's sliced through her like a pie.

Their faces hidden by cowls, twenty or so witches encircled them. Grace had no idea there were so many of them this close to the palace. Why hadn't they invited these women into their coven? Together they would be unstoppable.

Only then, as a leader separated herself from the pack and drew back her hood, she learned why.

The woman was hard to age, her face haggard through drink or work or both. Her name was Agnes Drury, and she *looked* like a witch, with her beady eyes and broken nose. An unfortunate time to resemble a hysterical etching. This woman could not glide through the halls of Hampton Court the way they did; a cruel thought, but a truthful one. Grace felt Cecilia inch closer to her side.

Agnes, however, had eyes only for Anne. 'You must forgive me, Your Highness. I don't know the proper ways to scrape and curtsy.'

'I am here as a witch, not as a queen.'

'In that case, you can fuck off,' Agnes said, and her coven split into a noisy gaggle of laughter. 'If we don't need you here as a queen, we definitely don't need you here as a witch. Middling. At best.'

'I know,' Anne said, drawing herself taller. 'That's why I need you.'

'You didn't need us in your fancy palace coven.'

'I don't control the palace,' Anne said. Grace kept her face neutral. That was only partially true. Since the coronation, Anne had brought many of her own women into her fold, although Cromwell kept her on a short leash. He had his spies everywhere. Gods, how he loathed Anne.

'What have you done for the likes of us?'

'I am trying, believe me, but the king is a man possessed. It is all he thinks of.'

Agnes's eyes narrowed. 'What is it you need, Anne Boleyn?'

'You know what I need, don't make me say it.'

'Oh I think I will make you say it. I want to hear it from your hallowed tongue.'

Anne steeled herself, her hands clenching into fists. 'I need a male heir.' Agnes looked satisfied. 'Can you help me?'

'You have a healer in court, do you not? Nan Cobbs?'

'She can't help me!' Anne snapped. 'I . . . I cannot seem to . . . '

Agnes softened, almost imperceptibly. 'We got healers, but none that could make a girl babe a boy. We can help you quicken, but that's all.'

'Lies. You lie.'

Whispers, a murmur, swept around the coven. Even Grace felt the mood change. An already dark night darkened. Agnes held up a hand to silence them. 'Oh, you don't want that sorta help, Your Highness.'

'I must.'

Agnes came closer, so close Grace felt her breath freeze on the winter night. 'There is ways a witch can get what she wants, sister, we all know that, but it ain't never worth the price. They take as much as they give.'

Grace took Anne's hand. 'Listen to her, Anne, for heaven's sake.'

Agnes nodded. 'Heed little Pretty's words. This won't end how you want it to end.'

Anne's eyes dipped. 'I have no choice. I'm running out of time.'

'Hush,' Grace said.

'I speak the truth. A boy. He has to have his boy.'

The women seemed to size each other up a moment, as if Agnes was trying to establish just how far Anne was willing to go. Grace already knew; she'd do whatever was necessary and more. Agnes finally spoke, low and even. The time for japery over. 'There is one. A powerful one. A son of Satanis, no less. But you wanna be careful, love, there's some what say this is all foretold. A son, born of a witch, will bring ruin to us all.'

'I don't have time for legends and stories, sister. If I can't give the king an heir . . . this was all for nothing.' Grace heard her voice tremble. The things Anne had done. The things she did still, and would continue to do. This degradation. It had to be for something, or it was nothing more than that. Perhaps she had spoken the truth earlier, and Grace did not know sacrifice as intimately as she did. Perhaps, after almost a decade of life in palaces, Grace had forgotten what it was to be a witch. She had been a lady so long, she believed there was such a thing. A lady is an artifice of lace and manners; of rouge and silk. A witch is of blood and sky.

'Very well,' Agnes sighed. 'And you're willing to do what you must? Mark my words, a great sacrifice will be demanded if this child is born. Always is.'

'Whatever it takes.'

Anne lay naked on the bank of the Thames, legs wide apart. The witches formed a broad circle around her. Agnes crouched before an altar of driftwood. She twisted the head off a dove and poured every drop from its neck into a shallow bowl. From deep in her throat, she muttered strange incantations. A summoning.

The rain started to fall, freezing cold. 'Are you making this happen?' Cecilia asked as lightning skittered across the sky like a spiderweb.

'No,' Grace told her.

Agnes took her cauldron to where Anne lay. Dipping her fingers into the dove's blood, she drew an intricate, looping symbol, the likes of which Grace had never seen, on Anne's abdomen. She continued, smearing the gore over her lap. Grace couldn't watch. It felt a betrayal somehow.

Thick cloud obscured the pale moon and the Thames grew darker.

'Lord Asmodai, hear me now,' Agnes yelled as lightning flickered wildly. 'Come unto me, your willing mistress. I beseech thee! Plant your seed within this woman. Child of Lucifer, make yourself flesh in her.'

A gale battered them all back. Cecilia clutched Grace tight. 'Grace, I am scared.'

Grace said nothing, but knew Cecilia would hear her fear over the howling winds.

'Stand strong!' Agnes screamed at her coven. 'This is a test!'

It rained harder and harder, until Grace felt something strike her head. Hail? It hurt. Only then did she realise the hail was moving. Toads. And frogs. Slick, squirming little bodies soon piled up around their feet, hopping around. The creatures descended on Anne's body and she closed her eyes, her mouth firm. A thick eel writhed over her collar, teasing her face.

'Stay strong, sister,' Agnes told her. 'You must be a worthy host. Prove yourself unto him.'

Grace bristled at the thought of Anne Boleyn having to prove herself to any man.

Then the downpour stopped, everything stopped.

'What's happening?' Cecilia breathed.

'Wait,' Grace said.

The brown waters of the Thames swelled. Something vast swam just beneath the surface; long, serpentine. Agnes turned to face the river. 'He heard us . . . ' Even she sounded surprised.

It was made from the riverbed itself. A shape rose out of the water, made of mud, and sludge, shit and silt. The creature had the tail of a great snake, but three malformed heads: one of a dragon, one of a calf and one of a ram. The air around it turned putrid. It was formed of filth and smelled like it.

The demon's liquid form shifted, shrinking as it made its way to the riverbank. It formed legs and a torso, the body of a muscular, lithe man. He wore no face, his features blank and expressionless, but he kept the curled horns of the ram. Asmodai, Prince of Lusts, said to have been carved from the cock of the demon king, Lucifer.

The demon strode towards Anne. Her Anne.

No, this would not do. Grace pulled her hand free from Cecilia and charged forward. She felt the air crackle and snap around her, building an arsenal under her skin. She would destroy it or die trying. She wasn't sure if the command, *stop*, came from her mouth or some other woman's lips, but it came out as a scream.

Anne opened her eyes and looked to her. A tear ran from the corner of her eye and into her hair. She held out a hand and

Grace felt an almighty punch to her chest. She was flung back, tumbling until she hit the earth. It hurt. She'd awkwardly hit her hip against some bricks or rocks. Wearily, she rolled over, just in time to see the demon descend on the woman she loved.

And that was when Grace understood that she loved Anne more than Anne had ever loved her.

NOW – JUNE 1536

· ◯ ◯ ● ◯ ◯ ·

LADY GRACE FAIRFAX

Hampton Court Palace - Middlesex

She returned to court by night. She wasn't sure, until that evening, that she ever would go back. It would have been easier by far to let them think her dead, but there was a lingering notion of words unsaid that had haunted her during her slumber. It was words unsaid that had led them here, after all.

For three blissful weeks she had lain dormant under the estuary at Southampton, healing, thinking, dreaming, reconciling the last ten years of her life. Chapters had come to her fully realised, as if she was living them all over again. Her first days at court to the last.

If only she'd been braver; if only she had, for even one brief day, seen them as equals in this world, she might have tried to stop Anne. Stopped the wedding; stopped the ritual.

Agnes Drury was the wisest of them all. January gone, the demonic child *had* been born: male, yes, but dead and deformed. She would never forget Anne's animal howl, cracking through the night.

Destiny had collected its spoils.

When she finally clawed her way out of the sandbank, it had taken Grace some time to realise she had come out of her hibernation *changed*. After hours, in a closed tailor's shop not far from the quay, she had first seen her new visage. Her body had rebuilt itself, but differently. Her hair was no longer white-blonde, but a fawn shade. Her face, once so angular, was softer, rounder. And her eyes were now warmly brown, like conkers. It was a less captivating face, and for that she was grateful. It was as if the earth had understood her desire to be anonymous to the world of men. She knew, had known since she was a girl, that beauty was equal blessing and curse.

After examining her face and body, not a wound or scar or burn anywhere to be found, she stole an unassuming pale dress and black cape. All that mattered was her ability to blend in. She would look just rich enough to move amongst courtiers if that was her desire.

Once clothed, she went to a darkened inn and raided their kitchen. She wasn't proud of stealing, but she needed fuel. All things in nature steal when they are forced. She took only what she needed for flight.

Then she made her way back to court. For peace of mind, if

nothing else. Truly, there was only one woman she wanted to see before she started her new life with her new face.

Margery, she said as she soared over Hampton Court. *Awaken.*

After only a few seconds, her hopeful voice came to her. *Grace? Is it you?*

They met in the chapel. Grace had asked her not to alert the others. She was still unsure if they ever needed to know she had survived the fire. Now able to control the flame, Grace lit a host of votive candles in the vestry with a wave of her palm.

Margery ran into the church, wearing only her chemise and a fur-lined cape. As she came close, she froze, no doubt observing her new face.

'It's me,' Grace said. 'Read into me.'

Margery looked her over once, and then nodded. 'But how?'

'I know not. I almost died. I sought refuge in the earth and water and emerged from my cocoon like this.' Her friend continued to gawk at her. 'I'm not sure it's my place to question these gifts, any of them.'

The candlelight flickered in Margery's wide eyes. 'And what of Cecilia?'

'Can I trust you?'

'You know you can.'

'Then she lives. She fled overseas.'

Margery went to speak but then reconsidered. 'It is for the best. Her death would have brought only a sip of spite and a lifelong aftertaste.'

'I quite agree.' Grace lit another candle and placed it at the foot of the Blessed Mary. 'Now. What of court?'

'It is said the new queen is with child.'

'Already? Gosh.'

'Lady Rochford plots against her.'

'Of course she does.' Grace sighed. 'Sweet Margery, I only came here to bid you farewell.' Margery was set to argue, but Grace cut her off. 'I have no desire to be part of another queen's household. I have even less hunger to see my wretched husband ever again. I believe that's why I was given this new facade, that I might finally be free.'

'But *wait*,' Margery said. She reached into her cape and withdrew a sealed parchment. 'This is for you.'

'What is it?'

'It was concealed in the frame of the portrait you stole.' Margery waited a moment for her to understand. '*That* was why she was so insistent you have it. Grace, she must have known. Maybe she sought counsel with the child seer, or perhaps she . . . just knew the king.'

Grace pressed the letter to her breast. 'Have you read it?'

'Of course not.'

It was addressed only to *G* and sealed with anonymous wax, no mark. Grace slipped her finger inside and unfurled the paper. She realised she had stopped breathing. This gesture was so very Anne. Of course she wanted the final word.

Grace read about half of the letter before she fell to her

knees on the cold chapel flagstones. Her stolen dress fanned around her, a creamy white rose. Grace pressed her words to her lips as the tears came, noisy, unpretty.

As she shook with sobs, she felt Margery's arms close around her and sank into her.

· ○ ◑ ● ◐ ○ ·

LADY GRACE FAIRFAX

Hatfield House – Hertfordshire

At first light, the coven met in the forests not far from the hall. The skies were clear, and it was going to be a favourable day, Grace could taste it. They all came: Margery, Jane, Temperance, Nan and young Isobel. And Agnes Drury.

'That's quite some spell,' Agnes said, regarding her new face.

'Not one I cast,' Grace said.

Lady Jane Rochford observed Agnes warily. 'Why are you here?'

'I was invited, thank you kindly, by the good Lady Fairfax.'

'Stop this tiresome bickering,' Grace snapped. 'We haven't much time. I'm expected at the house.' They listened keenly; no doubt intrigued by the vague invitation. Compelling enough that Grace Fairfax had cheated death, but to summon them to a forest at dawn felt clandestine, scandalous.

'Then explain yourself promptly,' Jane urged.

'I invited Agnes because she's a powerful witch, and you need her. You need every witch united against the coming storm. Ambrose Fulke will not be the last witchfinder, and his fervour is spreading. He is a martyr now. I apologise for that.'

'You rid the world of an odious man,' Margery said. 'Apologise for nought.'

'Nevertheless, the hunt for witches has only just begun. They are *organised*. You must organise too. No more rivalry and squabbles between disparate covens. There must be one almighty coven. Just as Anne foresaw.' Grace paused before going on. 'You must also open dialogue with the warlocks.'

'What?' Jane was aghast.

Grace held up a hand. 'They will side with whomever offers them the better deal. They could be a useful ally or a bothersome foe. Agnes's coven already trades with the warlocks. You can learn much from her.'

But Agnes looked confused. 'You say all this as if you ain't a witch anymore?'

Grace drew a fresh lungful of dewy morning air. 'I shall remain here. I . . . ' she paused, puzzling over how much to reveal. 'I have learned that the princess, Elizabeth, is a witch. It was her mother's wish that I remain at her side.'

Margery nodded. Jane seemed furious, predictably. 'And just how do you intend to explain your appearance?'

'Well, that's why I summoned you here this morn. I ask of

you a huge favour. Jane – you and Margery and Agnes are powerful enchantresses. I require not only a new face, but a new name, a new past, and new legacy. A lie that will fool everyone I meet. Can it be done?'

Jane shook her head. 'Grace, please. Come back to court. You are much needed there. Princess Elizabeth will never wear the crown. Listen to me; there's another. Anne's cousin, Katherine Howard, is a promising young witch. Quite exceptionally beautiful and ready to debut at court. We can have her on the throne in mere—'

Grace took her hands. 'Jane, stop this foolishness. I beg of you. Henry is a mad crocodile. In time he will eat himself, but for now, putting yourself in his path will only bring ruin upon your head. *Elizabeth* is the future.'

After a moment, Jane said. 'Then here we part, sister. The enchantment you ask of us is great . . . '

'Although made infinitely easier by the world thinking Grace Fairfax perished,' Margery said, stepping closer. 'It can be done.'

'It can,' Agnes said.

'So it shall be,' Jane said with genuine remorse. 'I shall miss you at court.'

The admission took Grace by surprise. The woman had feelings after all.

'And by what name shall the world know you?'

Grace had thought very hard about this. A name with connections to a good family with roots in many gardens; a trusted name; a name no one would question too closely. A name difficult to pronounce and spell.

She told them her new name.

The little girl, the princess, was all alone in the schoolroom. Such a tiny thing, with big blue eyes and porcelain skin. Her red hair was rebellious, refusing to sit neatly under her bonnet. She sat at a low desk, quite serene, watching the world go by outside the window. As Grace entered the room, she bowed her head. 'Your Grace.'

Fitting, she felt.

After a moment, the young princess said, 'Where is Lady Troy?'

'She will be here soon. I was to come and introduce myself. I am to be your new governess, Your Grace.'

By now, the three-year-old princess was more than used to the company of strange women. She merely looked her over. There *was* something about this little girl; an aura. Whether she was a witch or not remained to be seen. That part alone had been a lie.

'I knew your mother,' Grace said. 'Very well. It was her wish that I come here.'

The girl nodded, disinterested, and ran to a bookcase loaded with leatherbound volumes. 'These are my books.'

Grace joined her and crouched to meet her eye to eye. 'Is that so?'

'But I cannot read. I am only three.'

Grace smiled. 'You cannot read them *yet*. I shall teach you.'

'Can you?'

'Yes. That I can.'

'What's your name? My name is Elizabeth.'

'Oh I know!' Grace took her hand and pressed her forehead to her soft, warm skin. 'My name is Lady Katherine Champernowne.'

The little princess frowned.

Grace laughed at her politeness. 'Well, quite! Why don't you just call me Kat?'

'Kat!' The girl nodded and allowed herself a small smile.

And there they were. The child was safe.

· ○ ◗ ● ○ ○ ·

My Beloved

I can only pray you heeded my words and took the portrait.
Should this letter fall upon prying eyes, I have done my best to
protect you.

My love, you must go on. I had to die, that you could live.
They say I was a witch, but they saw me die as a woman. In the
end, the world had to see how powerless, how meek, how
penitent I was. And thus, we remain exactly how they need us
to be.

I owe you a thousand sorrys. I am guilty of ambition, and
love. I truly saw, on the crest of tomorrow, a world where I could
be me, and you could be you, and we could be together, just as
we are. Was I naïve? I wanted to change the world, and, greedy
fool that I am, I thought I would succeed. I believed, truly, that
once I gave him his heir, I'd be left alone. I would be free,
finally. He'd have his lovers, and I'd have . . . well, I'd have you.
You and Eliza. Together, we would be architects of a woman's
world, in which my precious daughter was worth as much as
any boy.

She is not of H. She is ours: yours and mine. When you held her that day, I felt it. We were a knot, tied forevermore. You must raise her, you must tell her about me, tell her about us. Tell her about all of us. Above all else, tell her she was loved, and she was wanted. I shudder to think what people will say about me, but let them. It's enough that you knew me.

I ask much of you, knowing beyond question there is none stronger, none braver, none with more grace.

This much remains true: I love you, and I always did. AB.

AUTHOR NOTE

· ○ ◐ ● ○ ○ ·

Lady Jane Rochford was beheaded for high treason at the Tower of London on 13 February 1542, on the same day as her cousin-in-law, the then-queen Katherine Howard.

Katherine Champernowne (later Ashley), known as Kat, became the royal governess to Princess Elizabeth in 1537, then lady-in-waiting, and eventually first lady of the bedchamber when Elizabeth became Queen of England in 1558.

In the succession crisis following the death of Henry VIII, Kat was instrumental in protecting the young Elizabeth from the intentions of treacherous Thomas Seymour and, later, her half sister, Mary.

In 1545, in her forties, Kat married John Ashley, Anne Boleyn's cousin. She was the queen's most trusted adviser, and the two were inseparable up until Kat's peaceful death in 1565.

Elizabeth continued to rule as queen for another thirty-eight years.

THANKS

$\cdot\ \bigcirc\ \bigcirc\ \bullet\ \bigcirc\ \bigcirc\ \cdot$

This book owes a great debt to the following people. *Queen B* wouldn't exist without my editors Natasha Bardon and Nidhi Pugalia. Thanks also to Kimberley Atkins and Kate Fogg for stepping in for a final round of edits. Thank you to the entire team at HarperVoyager in the UK and Penguin Random House in the US. Your support for the HMRC series is so valued. Holly MacDonald and Lisa Marie Pompilio deserve a special mention for their stunning cover art.

Thank you, Kim Curran, for being the most loyal friend and coming with me to Hampton Court. Thank you to all the staff at Hampton Court, the Tower of London and Hever Castle for answering my (many) questions about Anne.

Sallyanne Sweeney and everyone at Mulcahy Sweeney, thank you for everything, as always.

To all my friends, family, and dear, dear readers: I love you.

The coven will return in

HMRC:
HUMAN RITES

Her Majesty's Royal Coven

A Novel

At the dawn of their adolescence, four young girls took an oath to join Her Majesty's Royal Coven, a covert government organization established by Queen Elizabeth I. Now Helena is the only one still enmeshed in the stale bureaucracy of the HMRC: Niamh's a country vet, Elle is pretending she's a normal housewife, and Leonie started her own more inclusive coven. When a dark prophecy centered around a young warlock begins to unfold, the friends must decide where their loyalties lie: with preserving tradition or doing what's right.

"Superb and almost unbearably charming, *Her Majesty's Royal Coven* . . . expertly launches an exciting new trilogy."
—*The New York Times Book Review*

The Shadow Cabinet

A Novel

Niamh is dead. Her twin, Ciara, suffering from amnesia, masquerades as the benevolent witch as Her Majesty's Royal Coven prepares to crown her High Preistess. While Ciara tries to rebuild her past, she realizes none of her past has forgotten her, including her former lover, renegade warlock Dabney Hale. On the other end of the continent, Leonie is in search of Hale, rumored to be seeking a dark object of ultimate power. If the witches can't figure out Hale's machinations, all of witchkind will be in grave danger—along with the fate of all (wo)mankind.

"This entrancing mix of feminism, queerness, magic, and power-hungry villains makes for an intoxicating reading experience."
—*Nerd Daily*

PENGUIN BOOKS